THE RESUR
TREE
AND OTHER STORIES

Tony Cooper

First Edition

Cover by Xàos
kaosnest.daportfolio.com

TABLE OF CONTENTS

THE RESURRECTION TREE

Katy, 5 years old

"*This* is the church, and *this* is the graveyard."

Katy carefully placed rows of smooth grey and blue pebbles next to a half-buried red brick in the soil. She was squatting under the tree in her back garden, dressed in her best shiny black shoes, heavy black best coat, smart black school skirt and white shirt with black jumper and a grey scarf tucked in at the front.

Her parents were inside the house with the rest of the family. All of them in black. Still squatting, she turned her head, bunches sent messy by her coat collar and scarf, and looked through the glass sliding doors at the people standing around inside.

She had just been to see granny Flo "laid to rest" as father put it. She had been shushed quiet when she said "She won't get much rest in there." as she saw the uncomfortable looking box going in the ground.

She had only met her granny a few times. She had seemed nice enough, but once heard her mother say to her father that she was deliberately holding things up by refusing to go into a home. "But she's already *at* home." she had said, confused. Her parents ignored her, and she forgot about it. Now everyone was inside the house, still looking sad, which was odd as the sun had come out now, so it was nice. Her mother said she could go outside to play, but not to get herself dirty. Her brother was inside with them, made to say hello to everyone, go around with tiny sausages and open-topped pies. Nobody had wanted them from the table, so she guessed it must make them nicer if you go around handing them out instead.

She sighed and looked back down at her scene. The red brick had been there for ever, and couldn't be moved, so that became the church. She didn't have a pointy hat for it. Daddy said it was called the 'steeple', but that was a silly name as it was clearly a hat like the one bishops had.

She straightened up and started looking around the garden for a hat for the church. Daddy hadn't done much work to the bottom of the garden. The top half, nearest the house, had a narrow concrete patio, a small lawn that Daddy grumbled about mowing and some flower beds on either side. Halfway down on the right, the bed ended under the tree. It was a huge oak, taller than the house. It grew giant acorns in the summer, which her brother tried to knock off by throwing rocks at them, and went dead in the winter, only to come back to life again in the spring. That's why she called it the Resurrection Tree. Although her mother didn't like hearing her call it that. She said it was disrespectful. Only God could bring people back from the dead. And even then he had only brought one person back. That seemed like a waste to Katy, because people died all the time, so it would be nice if He brought them all back to be with their families again.

The bottom of the garden, past the tree, was overgrown with bushes and long grasses and weeds growing among them. An old barbecue lay on its side in there somewhere, a big rusty bowl on three thick metal legs. More red bricks, like that of Katy's church, were scattered around and would twist your ankle if

7

you didn't watch out for them. Katy had memorised where they all were, even in the long grass.

Bushes pulled at her coat as she made her way down the garden and she had to keep tugging herself free from them. She liked it down this end. It always smelled sweet and was cool on hot days. The neighbours' trees at the back and on both sides meant no-one could see in, so when she and her brother played here with their toys they could scream and jump around as much as they wanted, until their mother told them to shut up and play where she could see them. Then her father would be told to get it cleared so they could use it properly. She hoped he never would, as it was their secret den.

She was right at the back near the fence now. The collapsed rabbit hutch that had belonged to the previous owners was here, as was the small pile of compost bags, torn open, dark brown soil spilling out into the weeds.

It was there she found it, amongst the grasses, on the dark brown compost soil. A tiny dead bird. She could tell it was a bird from the beak and the few brown feathers still stuck to its wings, but the rest of it was bones. It was on its back, bony wing-arms stretched out, head turned to the side, beak open. It looked like it was sleeping, or waking up with a big yawn.

Katy smiled as she crouched down and picked it up. She walked back through the bushes, the bird cupped in one hand, stroking its bony head with the other, talking to it.

"It's OK birdy, I'm going to take you to the tree. He'll make you come back so you can fly again. I'm not going to put you in a box. That would be silly, you don't live under the ground."

She pushed her way back through the bushes onto the lawn and went straight over to the tree. Carefully, she laid the bird skeleton next to the red brick church, in the crook of two large roots.

"By the power of the Father, the Son and the Holy Spirit, fly again!"

She flung her arms up and wide, gazing into the snaking branches. After a moment, she looked back down. The bird lay still.

"Oh well, He's only made one come back, and that was a person. I guess He's not bothered about birds."

She turned back to her graveyard and decided to dig one space out for granny Flo. She should probably bury one of those tiny open-topped pies in there, as there still seemed to be plenty left.

As she stood up to go and get one of the pies, she heard a scraping noise. She froze. There was something scuffling around. Slowly, ever so slowly, she turned her head. Her eyes swivelled as far round as they would go and, through her bunches, she looked down at the ground to see the bony bird struggle to its feet. It wiggled its thin wing bones and fell over one of its feet that was bent all funny. Then it pulled its wings in, shook its head and looked up at her with tiny hollow eyes.

Katy scooped it up and sprinted over to the house, almost colliding with the doors. She screamed "Daddy! Daddy!" over and over as she pushed the sliding door open with her forearms, bird cupped tightly inside her hands. Everybody went quiet and looked at her as her father appeared from the middle of the room.

"Katy, what…"

"Daddy! Granny Flo doesn't need to be dead! We can put her under the Resurrection Tree and she'll come back like the bird!"

Her father sighed as he knelt down on one knee. Some others shook their heads. Someone said "Poor girl."

"Katy, we've talked about this. Your grandmother is with God in Heaven now."

"No, she's under the ground! We need to bring her to the garden so she can come back like the bird."

She slowly opened her hands.

Her father pulled his head back and someone said "Eww." as she revealed the skeleton.

He was about to tell her off when the bird shook itself and spread out its bony wings. Someone in the room screamed. Her father knocked it out of her hands and into the garden. He jumped out onto the patio and stamped on the bird, over and over and over. Katy yelled at him to stop, screaming that he was killing it again, that he was cruel. Her mother, who hadn't witnessed any of this, came rushing into the living room. Her father told her to take Katy upstairs as the bird, seemingly unhurt, tried to hop away across the lawn towards the safety of the bushes. Her mother called on God and the Lord Jesus as the guests in the house pressed themselves to the walls, talking in low tones, praying and staring at Katy.

With tears pouring from her eyes, she tried to tell them again that it meant granny Flo could come back, they didn't need to be so sad, but nobody took any notice. The last thing she saw was her father hitting the flailing bird with an old spade as her mother dragged her out of the room.

11

Katy, 8 years old

It was summer and Katy and Phillip were playing in their secret den behind the bushes. Daddy was at work while their mother busied herself inside the house, glad the children still played together and could entertain themselves. Truthfully though, they didn't play together much any more. He was four years older than her and spent most of his time with his mates from school, cycling around the area or just hanging out together.

So it was a rare day, like today, that he was with her. She had painted a cardboard box to look like a house and, with clumps of grass cuttings, created a small lawn at the front. Next to it sat her battered doll who today was "Joceline the Brave", risking life and limb to tear off into the dangerous woodlands nearby to rescue villagers in peril. Phillip was supposed to be the monsters in the woods. He had spent most of the time smashing the bushes with a branch of the tree that had fallen off in a recent storm and had ignored Katy's story completely. But she needed him now.

"OK Phillip. Joceline has saved the villagers and they're all in her house saying thank you. But now the big giant beast of the woods attacks the house, trying

12

to trample on it. DON'T TRAMPLE ON THE HOUSE! It took me ages to paint it. Just pretend you are, then I'll scare you away."

A flash of mischief crossed Phillip's eyes, then his shoulders dropped and he started pounding the end of the branch into the dry soil at his feet.

"This is boring."

"Well I didn't have to include you in the story at all! You can be bored somewhere else if you want."

Phillip rolled his eyes, stared at her, then shook his head before kicking puffs of dust towards the house and dolls.

"It's boring! Why do you still play at doll parties and adventurers anyway? You're too old for that now. You should be into clothes and bracelets like other girls."

Katy squeezed her eyes shut. Her mother said this all the time too, and she hated it. Whenever someone said it she felt a pain in her chest as if they were trying to tear her stories out of her. But she didn't let them. She swallowed hard and fought against the pain every time. She didn't care about clothes or jewellery. She would keep her stories.

"It's all stupid. It should be a bloke anyway. No woman has ever... rode into battle on a horse, or saved people from..."

Katy stood up straight, arms rigid by her sides.

"There's nothing wrong with having an active imagination! That's what Mr Willis says."

"Yeah, and Mrs Greaves says you need to stop daydreaming in class and pay attention or you'll never get a job."

"Who told?"

"No-one, I heard mum and dad talking about it.

"That's not fair, that's private!"

Phillip pulled his chin up.

"No it's not. Anything that happens in the house should be known by all of us. You can't keep secrets."

Katy shook with anger.

"That's not fair!"

"Well I'm going to tell mother I saw you playing with bones again, and you're going to get barred from playing out here again so you can go to your room and study and wear fashion and become a normal girl."

Tears balled up on Katy's bottom eyelid, "No, don't!"

Phillip grinned and ran away into the bushes laughing. Without even thinking what she was doing, she leapt after him, pushing him in the back to make him stop. She hit him so hard her wrists hurt, and they both fell to the ground.

Katy lay still for a while, winded. Then she pushed herself up to see her brother still lying down.

"I said don't you dare…"

He wasn't moving. She could only see his legs and lower back, the rest of him had fallen through a bush. She started to feel dizzy and tingly in the mouth and her lip trembled.

"Phillip, this isn't funny."

She knew something was wrong. He had messed around like this before, but something was different.

She couldn't walk between the bushes as she would have to step on him, so she walked around the side. As she came round she could see the top half of him. It looked odd, seemed to be hovering off the ground.

"Phillip?"

It was a long time before she moved closer and, when she did, she saw the rusty metal leg of the barbe-cue sticking into his head.

"No, no, no…"

She felt sick. This was her fault. But how could she have known? It was *his* fault for messing with her. She wouldn't have had to push him if he wasn't trying to

15

get her into trouble. She shouldn't have pushed him so hard, why did she do that? It was her fault. He was dead.

She started sobbing. She fell to her knees. From here she could see the blood dripping off his face. He was dead. She looked at her hands. They were the hands of a killer. She would go to jail for this forever. She would never get into Heaven. Not like Daddy's friend Geoff, not like granny Flo.

It was then she remembered the little graveyard she made under the tree for her Gran. Then she remembered the dead bird she found. Then she remembered the tree.

Wiping her tears away on her arm, she grabbed her brother's shoulders and pulled him up towards her. There was a scraping noise, a soft pop, then he became too heavy to hold and she dropped him. He twisted round onto his back.

There was a hole in his forehead the size of a two pence piece, just above his left eye, blood trickling out. It was black. It spread over his face like curling spiders' legs. His eyes were open, staring into the sky.

Katy whimpered at the sight, but she knew she had to press on. This had to work, it *had* to! She grasped the t-shirt next to his neck as tightly as she could and she dragged. She dragged him, inches at a time. She gritted her teeth and snarled as she pulled him through snagging bushes and over jagged red bricks. The bushes parted across her back as her hands slipped and she fell backwards onto the grass.

She twisted round and looked at the windows at the back of the house. Good, there was no sign of her parents. If they saw them like this they would panic and call the doctors and stop her moving him under the tree, where she really needed to get him.

She took hold of him again and pulled, heaved with every breath she had, until his bleeding head was between the two big roots of the tree. She knelt next to him, crying. She took his hand and said she was sorry. She wanted to say a prayer, but not like the one she did for the bird, a proper one, but she couldn't think of anything, she just hoped God was watching over her as the priest said he did.

Nothing happened. She closed her eyes, bowed her head into her chest, and waited for her mother and father to find them.

Then Phillip's back arched as he gasped in a lungful of air. He twitched around in the soil for a while, Katy holding his hand, until he finally stopped. Then he lay there, breathing, calming down, blinking blood out of his eyes, staring up at the branches.

It worked! The tree had brought him back. Katy was full to burst with happiness, then suddenly sick in her stomach: she was going to have to explain this to her parents and didn't know how, because she didn't understand it herself. All she knew was that it was all her fault.

He slowly sat himself up with Katy's help. As he did, a little gurgle of blood came from the hole in his forehead. He put a hand to it, felt the edges, started to put his finger into it before he quickly decided not to and looked at her.

"What happened?" he said.

"There... was an accident."

Katy, 9 years old

Katy, Phillip, and her parents were sat at the kitchen table. Her mother had cooked them beef stew and dumplings.

Phillip had a large square bandage on his forehead where the hole was. It didn't cause him any problems. The only outward sign there was something not right was a trickle of dark stained fluid from his nose every now and then. Other than that he was normal. Apart from the fact he looked exactly the same as he did the day of the accident.

Phillip ate his dinner hungrily. Except he never *felt* hungry any more, and food had no taste. He said it felt warm or cold, but there was no flavour, and that in any case it came out the other end the next day, looking the same as it went in. Katy hadn't wanted to know that. He stuffed half a dumpling into his mouth and smiled at her. He said it was just nice to have the feeling of eating and swallowing. That must be why Sandy still ate his food too.

The old Labrador was sat in the living room at the sliding doors. He had died months ago. Her father had found him curled up, cold, in his basket one morning. He said he wasn't surprised. Sandy was old and his back legs had started to go. Her father had considered taking the dog away and burying him in the woods somewhere, but he knew the first thing Katy would think of was the Resurrection Tree, and would force him to dig Sandy up anyway. So, reluctantly, they told her. They put him under the tree, and this time they all watched together as the dog twitched and scrabbled back into life.

That moment had changed how her parents felt. While her mother was still not ready to accept the tree could do this, she was willing to ignore her own concerns and feel blessed enough that her son was still alive and that Katy was happy to have both him and the dog back. Her father felt differently. Watching the dog jerk and whimper in the soil, seeing the soul sucked back into an unwilling body, made him certain it wasn't God doing this. He rarely talked to his son now, and when he did it was curt instructions or angry questions. The bare minimum of interaction. The boy he used to play football with, the boy he took fishing last summer, was dead. This abomination looked like him, and that was all. But, he could see his wife and daughter were happy, so he kept quiet, his foot anxiously tapping away.

The bone bird sat outside on the windowsill, huddled against the glass. After the dog came back, Katy had begged her father to tell her where the bird was. He said he had tried to put it in the rubbish but it pecked its way out of the bag, so in the end he buried it deep amongst the bushes. He dug it up and, sure enough, it was still alive. "Whatever alive meant", her father had said. Katy had washed it clean in the sink and used tape and thin garden wire to set its foot and wing bones in the right place.

It wouldn't go near her father. Even without eyes, it knew where everyone was and who they were. It preferred to stay outside where it could peck uselessly at insects and worms, although she had found it curled up with the dog in his basket a few times when the back door had been left open.

As for Katy, she felt she should have been happier. Her brother dying was her fault, but she made it right. She brought Sandy back because he was a lovely dog, and got on well with Phillip even after he died. Bone bird was for her, the first creature the tree brought back to life and she had to look after it. She had to look after them all, especially since her father wouldn't touch any of them. She couldn't quite understand how things could be back to normal and yet feel so different.

She had to admit to herself that Phillip had changed though. He didn't annoy her any more and seemed to be taking to the home schooling routine better than proper school. But there was one time when they were sat on the sofa watching cartoons, when out of the blue he asked her if she knew he could never have a normal life now. He said he wasn't get-

21

ting any older and he had a massive hole in his forehead. Neither would be good for his future job prospects, let alone being able to play five-a-side with his mates as they grew up.

Their parents had gradually withdrawn from any contact with his friends and their families and carefully hidden his 'condition', keeping everyone at arms length. Nobody came to call for him to go ride their bikes any more, and he had become quiet and thoughtful, the opposite of the old Phillip.

Katy couldn't solve that, but she said he could use make-up for the hole. Fill it with bandages and cover it all up like they did in films. His face screwed up at the thought, and a small glob of black blood oozed out of the hole. He said it was only girls that wore make-up. At least most of them did. He gave her a funny look when he said that, then turned back to the TV. Katy shut up.

There was one other odd thing. One day, when she came home from school, she saw Phillip, Sandy and bone bird sitting in a row on the grass in front of the tree, just staring at it. When she asked her mother about it, she said they had been there for hours and they often did that. She didn't like to disturb them and only called them in if the weather changed or it was time for study or food.

Whenever she or her parents quizzed Phillip about why they sat and watched the tree like that, he couldn't explain. He would go quiet and shake his head. Once, her father had become particularly angry, accused him of deliberately making things worse for them and that he *must* know what had happened. How could he *put* them through this and he had *better* tell them the truth. Phillip had screamed at him to shut up, that he didn't know. Then he barricaded himself in his room for days. Her father had become angry most of the time after that. Things at home had become difficult.

Phillip scraped the plate clean and started to slide off the chair.

"What do you say?" snapped their father, feet trembling.

Phillip froze mid slide and stared at him.

"Oh Arnold…", sighed their mother.

"What. Do. You. Say?"

"Please may I be excused?"

Their father looked at Phillip, disgusted at what he saw.

"Where are you going now, eh? You lot going to stare at that bloody thing for a few more hours?"

Phillip looked down at the floor as he stood up slowly.

"What do you do out there? Talk to it?"

"Arnold please! Leave the boy alone."

"No, I'm interested Patricia. I'm interested, particularly since he never tells us a damn thing about it even though he *clearly* knows what's going on. No, he prefers to keep secrets from us all. From his parents, even from his sister. The one who brought him back. Don't you think you owe it to her to explain what's going on?"

"Dad, it doesn't matter what he…"

"No…" her father dropped his cutlery on the plate and wiped his mouth. "Do you talk to it? Or does it talk to you? Telling you things?"

Phillip looked sideways towards Katy.

"I don't think it does Dad."

Her father held out his hand to her. "No, I want to hear it from *him*. For once. I want to hear from him. Does. It. Talk. To. You?"

Phillip was shaking now, breathing harder.

"You see, I bet it does. I bet it tells you loads of things you shouldn't know. Well I'll tell you something *you* don't know: we lock our bedroom door at night now."

"Arnold!"

Phillip looked up at him, puzzled.

"Want to know why? Because I think I know what that... *thing*, that evil thing out there tells you to do. It wants more, doesn't it?"

Katy looked on in horror. Her mother sat back, covering her mouth.

"It wants to bring back more of you. It wants *us* next, doesn't it? It wants you to kill us in our sleep so it can get more of you. So that we'll all be out sat on the bloody grass staring at it. That's it, isn't it?"

Phillip mumbled a quiet, "no".

"There it is. The first word out of your mouth about that tree since this all started and it's a LIE!"

His father stood up violently, sending his chair toppling over. He opened the back door and went out into the garden, muttering, "I'm done with this," over and over. Katy could hear him banging around in the shed.

Their mother stood up and slowly went to the door.

"Arnold, what are you doing?"

Their father came back into sight. He was holding an axe.

"I'm going to do what I should have done the moment I saw him." he pointed at Phillip.

Katy jumped up from the table and ran next to her mother.

"Don't kill him! Don't do it Dad! It's still Phillip. Please!"

Their father just shook his head and went over to the tree. He looked it up and down, sneering.

"I know what *you* are. You're just trying to tempt us aren't you? Tempting us with immortality. That's it, isn't it?"

"Dad?" Phillip gripped the edge of the dining table.

"Well I'm not having it. You're not taking over my family. You can go back to Hell where you came from!"

He hefted the axe behind him and twisted, swinging it into the trunk with a loud smack.

Katy and Phillip screamed.

"Dad no! Leave it! It brought Phillip and Sandy back! It's trying to help."

Their father ignored her as he swung harder and harder, exposing a scar of light beige wood. Each time he pulled away a spray of fibres scattered across the grass.

Phillip screamed. Sandy howled and started rolling around.

"THIS. EVIL. WILL. DIE." He swung harder and harder, jolting all the muscles in his back, but he didn't care. This would solve it. This would fix things. This would get them back to normal.

He only stopped when Katy tugged on his arm with all her weight. He was about to scold her for getting in the way of an axe, when he looked in the direction of her anxious pointing. He saw Sandy twitching through the sliding doors, a black smear down the glass. He turned towards the back door, looking into kitchen and could make out his wife on the floor with Phillip, gingerly stroking his hair.

"No. No no…" he dropped the axe and ran inside. He fell to his knees and pulled his son towards him. Through his t-shirt he could see black lines on the side of his chest, dark blood running down his jeans. Phillip was pale and gasping as he looked into his father's eyes.

"Don't kill me Dad. Please don't."

"Oh my son. My son." He let Phillip rest his head on his chest as he hugged his shoulders. "I can't do this any more…", their father wept as their mother placed her arms gently on his shoulders to comfort him.

Katy, 19 years old

"Ah yes, this argument again. The one where you wish I'd died even though I'm your son, but then say you still love me"

"You're neither dead nor alive. We can't grieve for you if you're still here. We can't move on."

"But I *am* still here. Still walking around and talking. Yeah, I've got a chunk out of my head, I'm stuck in a twelve-year-olds' body and I'm never going to have a normal life thanks to Katy... but I *am* here. You can't ignore me... although, to be fair, you've been doing a pretty good job the last eleven years."

"Oh, good to see you've learned sarcasm since the last time I saw you."

While their mother, Katy and Phillip sat around the kitchen table, their father stood at the door to the living room, leaning on the frame, still wearing his jacket.

They had split up the year after he attacked the tree. They had tried to take Phillip and the dog with them on a short holiday a few months before they separated. It was a weekend stay in a Cornish cottage. It was the first holiday they had been on since the accident and, as Katy realised many years later, the last time her father expended any effort to keep the marriage going. They had planned out every possibility apart from the one they couldn't know. Less than a mile from the house, Phillip started complaining of a headache. Their father had laughed and said, "See, you've got your sense of humour back already!". Two miles out and Phillip started convulsing. His body swelled up, his skin turned wet and translucent and twisting black veins of blood shone through.

Their father kept shouting, "No!", and hitting the wheel, until their mother forced him to pull over when she saw her son foaming at the mouth, his body sagging into the back seat like a melting jelly baby. By the time they parked up outside their house again, Phillip was almost back to normal. He hugged his knees to his chest, not letting anyone touch him. The dog, forgotten by everyone, popped its head up from the boot and nuzzled him. "Welcome home." their father had said, as he slammed the car door hard.

"Well *you* moved on fine Arnold." said their mother, bringing Katy back into the present. "You got that promotion. You could finally take that transfer you wanted. Oh, and you got a lovely young girlfriend out of it. Not a bad deal I'd say."

Their father stared at his ex-wife impassively.

"And what? You want me to be guilty about that, or do you just enjoy stating facts at me?"

"LOOK, there's no point going over all of this again, OK? I think we all know where we stand." said Katy.

"Yes. Right. Fine. So why did you call me here if it wasn't for a happy family reunion?"

Katy took a deep breath to calm herself.

"Neither of you deserved this to happen to you. None of this has been fair on you. It's driven us apart, what I did. Yes, I was only a child and didn't understand the consequences, but it was still my decision, so it's my responsibility. Phillip, Sandy and the bird are *my* responsibility now. Dad, I know you have to pay Mum a share of the mortgage as part of your settlement, but even so, I know it's hard on *you M*um to make ends meet. So, I want you both to sell the house to *me*."

There was silence until her father scoffed loudly.

"You? How are you going to pay for the house?"

"Professor Milligan has promised me a position on his research team when I finish my degree next year. I can do my PhD there."

"But how are you going to *pa-ay*?"

Katy shot her father a look that actually made him recoil in surprise.

"I have already spoken with several lenders who, with the job guarantee from the University, would be willing to lend me up to £220,000."

"WHAT? This place is worth at least three fifty!"

"Think about it this way: you can stop paying that extra mortgage money to Mum and she gets to save something at last."

"But I'll make nothing from it!"

"Let's face it dad, you never were."

He looked at Phillip. The dog stared at him from his basket.

"Jesus Christ."

"Arnold! I won't have blasphemy in this house."

A phone trilled in his pocket and he grabbed at it angrily. "God left this place well alone a long time ago." He tapped at the screen and shook his head.

"When?"

"When what?"

"The mortgage! When are you going to sort it?", he said, waving the phone in her direction.

"The best deal is from the one who want me to graduate first. So next May's earliest."

Her father tumbled some thoughts around in his head for a moment.

"Fine." He walked away through the living room. Katy followed him.

"So… is that all right then?"

"Hmm?", he was staring at the screen again.

"Ignore him Katy, I think his girlfriend is sending him a naked picture of herself again."

"Screw you!", he shouted towards the doorway, before turning back. "Yes, that's fine. Just send me the details when it's done and I'll sign whatever."

He looked around the living room and suddenly sagged. Katy thought he aged another ten years in that moment.

"Will be good to be rid of this place." He twisted his head to stare out at the tree. "And that thing."

He gave her a nod and in less than a minute she heard his car pulling away.

Her mother slowly walked up behind her from the kitchen. "Well, that was easier than I thought it would be."

"You know... you're not tied here Mum. I don't want you thinking you have to be here. You have a career too. And I want you to have a life after Dad. And us! Seeing as we're not going to be flying the nest."

Her mother shook her head.

"Kids live with their parents all the time nowadays...", she trailed off and went back into the kitchen, gingerly stroking Phillip's hair as she passed him.

Katy sighed. She was content a decision had finally been made. They now had a plan and she knew now the path the rest of their lives were going to take.

Katy, 73 years old

The cold grass tickles the back of my neck. The dark grey sky fills my vision, an endless shroud, infinitely far away. I could be falling into it and I wouldn't know. I don't panic. My straining heart doesn't let me.

Phillip and Sandy pull me along by the shoulders of my cardigan. I am light. It isn't a struggle for them.

I have often wondered what path our lives would have taken if I hadn't dragged Phillip under the tree.

Or if I hadn't pushed him as he ran from me. Would our lives have been happier?

Was I supposed to have killed myself under the tree, to join them? I did think about it, many times. My hesitation came from not knowing if the tree would *like* that. Whether it would accept someone who had taken their own life. So I never chanced it. I couldn't. If I truly died, then there would be nobody left to take care of my family. Not to mention the horrible possibility they would be discovered. The thought of what could happen to them kept me awake for many nights.

In the end, it came as I had hoped: a progressive disease with a measurable end point. I sought no medical help, no interventions. I have suffered these last six years terribly, yet I can't complain. I took it as some small degree of penance for what I did. Phillip would often say I should stop blaming myself, stop feeling like I should be punished. After all, what could an eight year-old me have understood? Who would have known it was even possible? But I took his life, then gave him back one that was barely worth living. I only brought back Sandy and the bone bird because I knew I could. None of them asked for it, so of course I blame myself. And yet, despite what I did, they looked after me. Phillip would help move me, wash and dress me, feed me. We would sit watching the news, reading books or just talk for hours. We all became good companions for each other.

We had to after mother died. Cancer took her in the end. She was only sixty two. She helped look after us, even though we told her many times she had to get on with her own life, not stay tied to the life *I'd* chosen. But in a way we were happy she stayed; it kept things normal. Even so, she was never entirely comfortable around Phillip. The little jump when she noticed he was suddenly close to her, the long pauses after he spoke as she pulled his words apart, trying to find some hidden meaning that would help her understand. I could see she was torn. On the one hand she loved him because he was her son, but on the other she was terrified of him because she didn't know what he was.

My father... well, I don't know if he was *ever* happy. He never forgave me, but the closest he came was in the hospital not long before *his* heart gave up on him. He begged me not to put him under the tree, said he didn't want to come back. I got angry, said I'd never even considered it and told him I wasn't a stupid little girl any more. He smiled at me, said, "That's my

Katy." We talked for over an hour after that, almost a normal conversation, until he got too tired and I left him to sleep.

And now *I* am getting ready to sleep, but with the knowledge I will return. It hasn't made the thought of death any less terrifying. It is still an end point. But I know for sure there is something after. It isn't the traditional afterlife, that which awaits those who die normally. This is a different afterlife, a death without divesting yourself of the responsibilities of this world, but accepting them completely and moving on with them by your side. My responsibilities.

Phillip. Sandy. Bone bird. They sit in a row on the grass, watching me. Watching the tree. In all this time I have never lain here, never saw what they saw at their moment of return. I didn't think it would be right. Now I look up into the branches of the tree and see the path of all our lives, dividing forever... and I know. I know I will finally be with them.

THE CHAOS POLICE

He looks nervous. He should be. He's killed seventeen people in the last twelve years, and now we have him.

I stare at him through the two-way mirror as he keeps rechecking his watch, keeps adjusting his tie, keeps brushing his drooping fringe back into his messy hair. He looks dreadful. According to him, he was on his way to a job interview when our officers picked him up. An interview? Like that? Looks like we have prevented an HR disaster waiting to happen.

No Vanessa, too flippant. Even for a thought. We've prevented much more than that.

My boss gives me a nod and wishes me luck as I take a deep breath, leave the observation room, and step next door. The man immediately spins round in his chair and gets up.

"Look, I've already been here for half…"

"Sit down Mr Henderson. My name is…"

"I am LATE for an INTERVIEW! And you KNOW I haven't done anything wrong, otherwise I'd be at the *other* station down the road!"

"SIT. DOWN… Mr Henderson."

A fight-or-flight moment dances in his eyes before he sits heavily, sighing and shaking his head.

I smile and take a seat, placing my paperwork and tablet on the table.

"My name is Detective Barker. In a moment I will begin recording this interview, but I would just like to reiterate that you have a legal right for a counsellor to be present and if at any time you wish to stop the recording, please say so."

"I don't need anyone else, because I won't be here long."

Arrogance born of irritation and frustration. Oh dear, we've interrupted his terribly important, chaotic life.

"Recording start."

A small, flat screen slides out of the wall next to us. It lights up, showing two CCTV camera views of us, a red "Recording" symbol and the time and details of the occupants of the interview room.

"Interview of Mr James Henderson by Detective Vanessa Barker. Eight-forty-three am. Twelfth of May twenty sixty two. Suspect was advised of his rights and the charges against him at the time of arrest. Can I just confirm your details first sir: your full name?"

He looks at me like he's ready to spit.

"James Benjamin Henderson."

"And your address?"

"Flat twenty-three-A, Gardiner Court, Fir Tree Avenue, Dudley."

"Thank you. Now. Do you know why you have been brought here today Mr Henderson?"

"Of course I don't. That's how this bullshit works isn't it?"

It was always said it was pointless looking for someone to blame when accidents happened. It was said there was a multitude of factors involved: it was the fault of systems not individuals, it was herd mentality disrupting individual agency, simply too many elements outside of our control, and so on. Thankfully a group of scientists ignored this defeatist thinking. Led by Professor Dijkhausen at the University of Amsterdam, his team created ERIS. It was a computer system that used multiple data analysis methods on both manually-entered data, from good old-fashioned detective work, and data scrubbed from social media platforms to establish patterns of causality. As a test, they went back through a year's worth of serious accidents and the further they dug back into the reasons why things happened, they found convergences. Convergences on certain companies, specific people and decisions they had made. The better the data, the better the results.

It took many years to convince any authority of the worth of this sort of data analysis. If it couldn't help them find terrorists, they weren't interested. At least they weren't to begin with. Then in 2051 a tired driver overturned his coach full of schoolchildren on the M6 as he jerked the wheel to stop himself drifting onto the hard shoulder. Professor Dijkhausen's team used ERIS to analyse the driver. Every news report, every police interview, court proceedings, his entire internet history, the lot.

That's how they found, "Causality Catherine", as she was dubbed, a sociopathically selfish woman who had kept the driver talking in a webchat until 5am that morning. She knew he hadn't slept yet and was to start work at 6am, but she didn't care. She wanted someone to talk to, and that was all that mattered. Now, if that had been the only link to her, there may have been a single, frothing tabloid piece outing her, calling for her to be charged with something, and then no-one would ever have heard about her again. But that's where the analysis came in. They found links to a workman who reversed his digger over a colleague, a teacher who fell asleep at the wheel and killed himself, a pilot who caused a near-miss at Stansted airport and dozens upon dozens more. At first they thought that they had made a mistake, that the data was wrong, but in the end her behaviour had led to over thirty deaths and serious injuries over the course of dozens of accidents.

They went public. The news played clips of her webchats, where the men would all try to disengage, telling her they needed sleep, only to have her face tighten and scream, "But I want to talk!", before suddenly becoming warm and loving again, and continuing her conversation. In the end it was the combination of media pressure and the sheer number of links to accidents found by the alpha version of the system that convinced the UK government and police of its worth.

Today, whenever an accident occurs, we conduct an enormous amount of research and interviews. All

data is logged into the latest version of our ERIS su-
percomputer, which combines this information with
its own data mining algorithms and teases out links
and relationships into one giant spiderweb of events.
The key is to look for, "bright spots", where multiple
threads overlap. Of course, we find lots of genuine
criminals this way, but what *we're* interested in, and
what the original creators of the system were really
looking for, are those people who have no idea their
actions are disrupting others' lives. So called, "silent
actors".

They fall into two types: Type I tend to lead chaotic
lives, with little or no organisation or planning, falling
from one crisis to the next, always wondering why the
world is against them. Their actions are like randomly
hurled stones into a pond, multiple waves overlapping.
Type II, on the other hand, tend to be sociopaths who
actively manipulate those around them for pleasure
and personal gain. Their actions result in slowly ex-
panding ripples from the same locations, other people
being tipped into chaos by proxy.

This guy is a Type I. The type who gets frustrated
by his own frustration, yet does nothing to change his
behaviour to counter it. Like his current inability to

conceal his irritation when it would be socially benefi-
cial to do so.

"You Chaos Police are just a bunch of frauds! You
can't prove anything you charge people with, it's all
bollocks!"

"Causality Corrections Agency."

"What?"

"'Chaos Police' isn't our official title."

"I don't care! Look, just what the hell am I supposed to have done?"

I tap a button on my tablet. "I'm glad you asked," I
smile. "Henderson, James B., charges sheet." The wall
display loads the list and I start reading.

"On 03/09/50 shouted at Mrs Brianna Hawkins, a
checkout assistant at ASDA, saying she was slow and
too old for the job, causing Mrs Hawkins physical distress..."

"Physical distress!?" he spits incredulously.

I stare at him until his face takes on a more contrite
look and I continue. "...causing Mrs Hawkins physical
distress, causing her to ask to leave work early as she
was feeling ill, causing her to be driving her vehicle
home along Appleby Drive at three thirteen pm when
she had a stress-induced heart attack, causing her to
veer onto the pavement and run over and kill two

THE RESURRECTION TREE AND OTHER STORIES

schoolboys and seriously injure their mother and baby sister."

"Oh... Christ."

"On 22/04/54 knocked Mr Arnold Caldwell when running down the escalator at New Street Station, causing him to spill coffee over the jacket of Miss Aisha Turner in front of him, causing a heated argument between them which, incidentally, was not resolved by him mentioning it wasn't his fault, causing Mr Caldwell to arrive at his place of work, Xemos Engineering, stressed and distracted, causing him to overlook a pressure sensor reading on the piece of equipment he was working on, causing an explosion that killed him and a co-worker instantly, and starting a fire that claimed the life of another engineer, and further causing the death of a fire-fighter who was attending the blaze when a piece of roofing fell on him.

On the same date, Miss Turner had to take a detour on her way to work to buy a clean jacket, causing her to be running across crossing Hadfield Road at eight oh-seven am when she was struck by a taxi, resulting in multiple head, chest and pelvic injuries, causing her to die two weeks later in hospital from a stroke caused by a blood clot due to immobility from her injuries.

On 15/05/55, took the last sandwich from the shelf at the Boots at Heathrow airport departure lounge, causing an argument with a Mr Jaques Armand who claimed he was reaching for it, causing Mr Armand to carry that anger onto his flight, causing him to drink heavily until he became abusive and physical with staff, causing the plane to return to the airport where he was arrested and taken off the plane by police.

On 14/07/57 while at work, had an argument with work colleague Mr Brian Davies, causing him to commit suicide later that week."

"No, that wasn't my fault. The guy had other problems... please, I can't..."

I ignore him and continue. He has to hear this.

"On 12/12/60 tweeted a deliberately provocative tweet about the lack of defending prowess of Tottenham Hotspur football club, causing Mr Kevin Johnson to definitively decide that the time was right to teach the fans of Wolverhampton Wanderers a lesson at that night's match, causing him to glass Mr James Bailey in the neck during a multiple-person fight near the ground, causing Mr Bailey to die from blood loss before he could receive medical attention.

On 28/03/62 played loud music until early that morning, causing your then neighbour Mr Hardeep to sleep in, causing Mr Hardeep to be late for his works bus, causing a ten minute delay to departure, causing the driver of the bus, Mr Alan Morrison, to speed and make rash driving decisions in order to make up time, as the private bus company he worked for had to pay penalty fines if they were late delivering staff by more than fifteen minutes on two occasions a month, causing Mr Morrison to pull out into the middle lane of the M5 from between two lorries into the path of a removal van pulling back into the middle lane from the outside lane, causing a pile-up that claimed eight lives, and injured over a dozen more.

Total: seventeen fatalities, six permanently disabled, twenty-five serious injuries."

I pause before I look at him. "That last one was the incident that allowed us to make the final link. The others were confused by technical enquiries, various product and machinery safety assessments, twitter noise etc. The moment we ran the works' bus data through our system, one bright spot lit up that linked all of these events together. You."

He stares like a rabbit in headlights at the unequivocal data in front of him, the debris trailing behind his path through life.

"And these are only the accidents we can link together within a legally defined probability limit. There are over fifty more 'faint' links from age seventeen until now."

It only takes moments for all the typical arguments start pouring out. "How was I to know?" "Not fair." "Not deliberate." "Not directly responsible." "Can't prove it."

I let him rant through his denial phase. I wouldn't mind, but his causality history clearly shows him to be too much of a danger to be allowed to make his own life choices. If it isn't obvious to him after hearing that charge sheet then... no, I understand.

I only get it because of our mandatory psychology training. The truth is he *does* understand, it's just his reaction to suddenly having his sense of agency taken away from him. No-one likes to be presented with information that conflicts with their internal version of the world. Their first reaction is denial. This is an often aggressive self-defence mechanism, especially apparent in social media. Little bubbles of self-affirming worldviews form, that react with vitriol whenever they bounce off each other. Online, like-minded people hand out boiler-plate counter arguments to use as shields so that no intellectual effort has to be spent processing any conflicting information. In here however, we have real-world evidence. Threads of disaster hang off everyone we bring in, and we show them whether they want to know or not. Because they have to know. They have to see. We don't let them get away with not understanding.

So whenever I am told that it's not fair to lock up innocent people who have committed no crime I tell them it's not fair that innocent people who have committed no crime are killed through the deliberate or unwitting recklessness of others. We're just restoring the balance.

He is silent now. Re-reading the list. Looking at the names of the dead.

"How... how was I supposed to know about all that?"

"You weren't. That's our job, to find out."

He has stopped fiddling with his watch. His hands are clasped together tightly, trembling as he stares at them, eyes out of focus.

"So what... what do I do now?"

"Absolutely nothing. By law. You will now be remanded in custody for the safety of others until your hearing date at which your Social Conditioning Plan will be finalised for you."

He looks up at me.

"But I can change! If there something I'm doing that I can stop doing to prevent all this, then I'll do it!"

"And you will. You will have access to full Social Safety Conditioning including life planning, decision making and outcome awareness and when your treatment is complete, and only if we can be sure your actions will be more controlled, you will be released under monitor for two years, the standard length of time it takes us to fully assess your onward causality risk to our satisfaction."

"I'm going to prison?"

"No. You haven't committed a crime Mr Henderson, but you will be held at a secure treatment centre under Section 8 of the Causality Corrections Act for the duration of your Social Conditioning Plan."

"But I've got a job interview I'm supposed…"

"Which you're going to miss." I shake my head. "Which you were already late for weren't you?"

"What? Well, only a few minutes…"

"You were going to run across pedestrian crossings that weren't safe to cross weren't you? Going to push through crowds, getting frustrated at other frustrated people? How many direct accidents would that have caused? And of those people, how many with heart conditions who had to brake suddenly to avoid you, or get a shock from you barging past them? How many would have fallen, unstable on their feet. How many would have carried that transferred anger and frustration into their own social situations, like a fistful of stones hurled into a pond?"

He stares at me, blank eyed, only barely grasping what I'm saying.

"Don't you see Mr Henderson? You're a danger to others. That's why we are removing you from society for treatment, for the safety of the public. Our job is to make sure you fully understand how dangerous you are and how to fix yourself, so that you never harm another person again."

I lean forward.

"Do you understand how dangerous you are Mr Henderson?"

***

My boss praises me for a very efficient and complete debriefing as Mr Henderson is escorted away for processing. It won't hit him properly until he has spent a few nights in the treatment centre. It will suddenly dawn on him that he could be here for many,

many months. At least he's a Type I, he should come round soon enough. It's the Type IIs that are the worst, who react angrily, often violently. Some have spent years in secure assessment, refusing to acknowledge they are a derailed train, crashing through other people's lives.

Because of the nature of our job, we can't know how many lives we have saved, or who they are. But we do know the incidence of serious accidents has dropped in the eight years the programme has been running, by a small, but statistically significant amount. It took some time, but the data is winning our argument. The US and Germany are looking at our technology, looking to start their own programmes.

Some say we're picking on clumsy people, that the people we send to the rehabilitation centres are not criminals, just unlucky. Of course there is risk in everything. I have a risk of causing an accident. Incredibly low however. My assessment on application put me at the 4th centile, in the bottom four percent of the population for onward causality. But for those on the 90th centile upwards, for those we know are causing deaths and accidents, are we just supposed to ignore them? Shrug and say, "Hey, accidents happen!", when we know that we can save lives by giving these people new life skills, making them better people?

When you *can* do something, you should. There is no maybe about it.

I sit down at my desk, log into my terminal and prepare the paperwork for Mr Henderson.

Ultimately, what we're doing here is not making criminals, we're making better people. And that's why I do what I do.

***

Current watch list calculations complete

[ACTION] Updating risk visualisation systems...

ERIS system refresh...

[TASK] 1208_12.05.62: Recalculate causalities for CCA staff

Current CCA staff calculations complete

[NOTE] 1 on CCA staff watch list with statistically significant risk change

[DATA] Detective Vanessa Barker +1.4, now 23rd centile onward causality

[DATA] Risk increased by greater than 0.4 percent-iles/week for 4 week period -

Action point trigger reached

[DECISION] Alert staff member - HELD
[DECISION] Alert line manager - HELD
[DECISION] Monitor staff member - GRANTED
ERIS system refresh...

JAZZ ON THE RADIO

"Attendance records for last month? We need them Professor!"

The shrill pronouncement momentarily rescued Professor Taylor from his clumsy tumble dryer of thoughts and dropped him, confused yet grateful, in the middle of the Student Services Department. The loud clattering of keyboards, distracting background hum of collected technology and random musical chimes from concealed mobiles put him firmly in the College Student Services department

"Pardon me Carol?"

The girl was stocky with short bleached hair and a beefy masculine face. He surmised she must only have been in her early twenties, but looked older. She wore a turquoise off-the-shoulder deep V-neck jumper that

revealed a bra strap and remarkable cleavage, a pair of tight hipster jeans that revealed a distressing amount of belly flesh and an array of small, cheap tattoos peering out from underneath both that revealed most of her personality. He was always amused at how girls failed to see that just because they wear the same clothes, it doesn't physically turn them into the models that advertise them. She was also holding a pink, clear plastic folder in her hand, which she waved vigorously to emphasise the seriousness of his situation.

"You're late with your class records again. We need to put these on the system for the monthly management meetings. And I'm not Carol, my name's Pam."

Complete bewilderment danced between his wild eyebrows as the external world failed to match his internal version. He used a stubby forefinger to push his glasses up to the wrinkles between his eyes and stared at her.

"Carol left last year? Remember?" An unsaid 'You silly old man.' dangling on her mental tongue.

The Professor looked down and deeply scrutinised a small area where two carpet tiles didn't quite meet at the corners.

Carol. Pam. Similar clothing. Similar hairstyles. Similar attitude. Hard to tell anyone younger than forty apart nowadays he mused. Student Services were the worst, all young females employed to do nothing but quiz him about figures, numbers, costs, scores, attendances, as if constructing a giant equation to solve a problem they couldn't describe.

Seemingly abhorring any kind of reflective silence like most people her age, Pam repeated her question. Unfortunately he could find no space amongst the storm of unsorted thoughts inside his head, so he sought a retreat instead. With a dismissive wave of the hand, a "Right!" of mixed certainty and a confident start towards the door, he was off.

"Professor Taylor!"

The motor in his mind had already given him momentum towards his new destination, so this was an unwelcome false start.

"What is it?" he barked, hunched back still presented to his verbal assailant.

"We need those records *now*!"

"Ah, just make them up," he grumbled.

A titter of female laughter breezed through the room as Pam fizzed.

"I can't just make them up..."

57

"Why not, that's what I always do!", ended the conversation as he stormed out of the room propelled by the flapping tails of his tweed jacket.

As he barrelled through the throng of inert students decorating the corridors, something about a bill flashed across the back of his eyes like a red sock spotted in a white wash. He stopped abruptly, a tuft of swept-over silver hair dropping across his forehead.

He foraged rapaciously in all his pockets, sending squealing toffee wrappers and strands of tobacco fleeing. Finally he pulled a crumpled, once-folded, then rolled up letter from an inside pocket. He unravelled it thoughtfully, like a lost parchment, only when it was fully opened proclaiming it a Gas Bill. A red one too. Urgent. "Yes, yes." he mumbled to himself, "'ll in good time."

As he re-folded it, he couldn't help but notice the envelope window. Once clear, now a cloudy white smashed up windscreen. It crackled as it formed and collapsed, sending shards flying into his face.

"No. He swayed slightly as his mind spun, old memories buffeting him. Sweat formed on his brow. "Not again…"

***

The memory always starts well. Laughter. Contagious laughter in the air, Jazz on the wireless in the car as you careen down tar black country lanes, headlights scything through the darkness.

She is sitting in the passenger seat, waving her hands in time to the infectious music, slapping the dashboard, bracelets clashing like tiny cymbals. Her eyes are closed, creased from laughing, cheeks flushed from just a little too much brandy. You are a lucky man indeed Alfred.

You have just been to a dinner party at the invitation of your new boss. You had finally found a teaching position with prospects and the "right kind" of colleagues. As was traditional, all staff met before the new term at the headmasters' country house for dinner and drinks and to consecutively one-up each other with tales of their Summer Exploits in far away countries. You willingly joined in and your story of a poor, newly graduated, soon to be wed couple slumming it in Blackpool raised as many guffaws as it did unimpressed eyebrows.

Your laughter now is the release of the pent up giggles over Mr Bradley's wife's hair, which had spent the best part of the evening trying to escape it's cranial prison by sliding down behind her left ear.

Yes, always the laughter first. Then the expletives as you look away from her to find the windscreen filled with bushes and thin tree trunks. The headlights scour them of colour, like crazed chalk marks on a blackboard. You don't even have time to brake. Then comes the screams, tearing of metal, thrashing and snapping of wood, dashing of broken glass across your face, then silence save for the slowing squeak of a wheel turning freely. Cold air blows across your face, and branches creak in the darkness.

You call her name. There is no reply. It is too dark for your eyes to adjust to and you can't move your legs or left arm. You can feel them though, sharp irregular blades painfully protruding into your shoulder and hips. You call her name again quietly. No reply.

Then the other car pulls up at the void by the road-side and the harsh chemical light smothers the cabin.

She is halfway out of the windscreen, legs twisted like roots to somewhere under the dashboard. Her skirt lies inappropriately high on her thighs, revealing the suspenders you didn't know she was wearing. The cream mohair coat seems to be several sizes too big on her shrunken frame. An arm is bent awkwardly in on itself across the bonnet. Her pearl necklace is stained black with blood and sparkles incongruously. Her eyes are wide open to the world yet see nothing.

You grow angry. You struggle to move as you hear voices pushing through the undergrowth. You can't let them see her like this. You must fix her skirt down, smooth her hair, close her eyes. But you can do nothing. You sob with pain and despair. You call her name and pass out.

***

"Catherine."

"Professor?"

"Eh? What?"

The memory began to sink back in with the rest of them as he found himself sitting at his desk in front of the class of students. In his hand was a muted colour Polaroid of her standing on Blackpool pier, holding two ice creams and a handbag.

"Professor?"

He looked up into the face of a young African girl, her large eyes full of concern. "The class is here now?"

"Right!"

He looked out over the young faces staring at him and motioned the girl to sit down. He placed the photo back in the top drawer, and stood up to bring the class to attention.

"Today we are carrying on with neurotransmitters from last time..."

"Professor...", interrupted a disembodied voice, "we finished that last week? We're on to sensory coding now?"

There was a ripple of giggles.

"'Of course we are!"

He found himself still staring at the photograph, drawer half open, hand uncertainly stroking the handle.

"Open your books to page... to the appropriate page, and we'll start!"

He took a deep breath and closed the drawer shut

SEAVIEW HOTEL

By the time I arrive at the hotel the sun has long since finished it's daily purging of the landscape, and moonlight licks the hills.

The hotel is a sturdy three storey granite block building. It looks like it has been standing here forever. I imagine that such an exposed part of the Scottish coast requires something this solid. It is, however, ruined by the very modern extended lobby that protrudes from the flank of the building into the gravel car park, an ungainly structure made entirely of glass and steel. The two eras intertwine uncomfortably. As I face the entrance it glows from within, like a huge glass furnace dug into the hillside. Behind me the night is still, save for the gentle murmur of waves down by the shore. The tide is full in tonight. By tomorrow morning it will be full out again.

With the gravel crunching underfoot I wave my case to activate the sliding doors and enter the lobby. The stench of freshly glued carpet tiles, drilled wood and plastic assaults my senses. Once I become accustomed, I feel a raised heartbeat, taste the sweat of discomfort and feel the eyes gladly welcoming me to the desk.

"Welcome Sir. Sorry about those doors, some o' our guests have bin having problems wi' 'em the night." I cannot help but smile at her delightful Scottish twang as I feel her heart slow.

I'm about to reply, but I am interrupted.

"So you're ignoring me are you?"

The other guest in the lobby leans on the desk, staring down the girl. We both know each other instantly. I can tell he has been haranguing her for some time. I sigh inwardly. I had hoped for us to remain as inconspicuous as possible. I now have greatly lowered hopes.

"Mr Vilmus," I say, "I hope you aren't harassing the staff already."

I am certain he was wearing the same clothes the last time I saw him. Battered denim sleeveless top, decorated with buttons and badges, felt pen and ink scrawls of logos, faces and swear words. Black combat trousers, faded to charcoal with wear. Black, battered, thick soled boots, laces half tied. His arms are covered in various vile tattoos. Woven fabric bracelets and fat rings scrunch up his wrinkled skin. Fingers stained brown with decades of tobacco.

He turns round slowly, deliberately, as if mulling over an insult. Then his draped curtain face parts in a manic smile.

"Mis-ter C!" He bends back, arms and legs apart, welcoming his old friend.

I make no movement and in the end Vilmus clasps my shoulders and stares intently into my eyes.

"We both made it."

"We most certainly did."

Vilmus laughs maniacally then turns back to the now puzzled girl and points a finger at her.

"I was just telling this gorgeous piece of arse here about our little weekend. You know, our friends an' all that. Here. By the sea."

"Were you indeed..." I turn to the girl, hoping he kept to the script. "I'm Mr Caldwell, I'd like to check in please, and forgive my friend here. He's somewhat lost in time."

"Aren't we all Mr C. Aren't. We. All."

With that he gives an exaggerated conspiratorial tap to his nose and saunters off towards the bar like a sailor at sea. Vilmus is a tsunami of personality, gathering up in his wake those like him and drowning the weak. I can't deny that his charisma is still magnetic, even through the smothering blanket of decades of alcohol and drug abuse.

The girl studies the old punk carefully before turning to get the reservations book. I carefully smell her. She has the aroma of flowery fabric freshener, mint chewing gum, an older man and a faint, overly synthetic perfume.

"Ah yes, Mr Caldwell, you're the group organiser I believe? I'm te ask ye wither there's bin any cancellations or changes ye know about?"

I shake my head. "Have any others arrived yet?"

"Just Mr Trier… weiler?" I nod. "And Miss... Ser, Kser..." She looks at the computer monitor and frowns intently.

"Czerwinski."

"Aye, her. And Mr Vilmus of course." She glances at the clock.

"Yes, apologies for the lateness of our arrival, which is somewhat dictated by our means of travel." I hand over a credit card. "This is for all the group's expenses during our stay, including the bar which I'm sure my friend will be draining dry." The girl smiles, finally relaxing in my presence, and secures the card in the till. She slides a form across the reception desk for me to fill in, then turns around and grabs a room key from the pigeon-holes behind her.

"Many other guests tonight...?" I glance at her name badge, "Kelly?"

"We're about half full actually, so no bad fer this time o' year."

"Perfect."

***

The mahogany bar stinks violently of the thousands of drinks served across it. Vague landscapes painted with little skill and even less effort hang on the walls, apart from one which appears to be an original James Norie. In their ignorance, the owners have hung it directly above a radiator, and the lower colours have taken on a rich yellow sheen. Nonetheless, it is still worth more than their new lobby. Ceilings, walls, floors, windows and furnishings all seem to have travelled from different periods in history and decided to settle in the same spot. A final destination for furnishings lost in time.

We are all gathered in the corner of the bar and a visibly annoyed young barman hovers behind the pumps. I'm guessing he had hoped for a quiet night chatting up the receptionist, but instead got Vilmus forcing him to open every bottle.

I look around at the group. Eight of us in total. I am somewhat surprised they all came.

By the fireplace stand a terrified young couple, recently turned, the horror of the reality of everyday survival newly etched into their faces. They stand apart from the rest, cautious of these new animals they make company with. They will be gone by morning.

Sitting nearest to them, in an armchair, is a large man in a suit and tie with swept over blonde hair, round glasses and a goatee. He gently sips an expensive wine. He must be the German.

Another couple sit on the sofa next to him. An older woman and her younger sire. They chat intermittently, not looking at each other. They are just sick of it all. The weariness drips off them both.

Then there is Emelia, among us but alone, staring into the middle distance. I cannot read her at all.

Last, but never least, Vilmus is at the bar, investig-
ating the hotel's range of whiskies.

All but two of us have followed the contemporary
dress code for this first night. Vilmus stands out in his
outrageous punk clothing, hair and piercings. Emelia
sits among us in the same way a bronze sculpture sits
in the middle of a flowing crowd. A timeless artefact,
impervious to change. She is wearing a rich maroon
and gold original Elizabethan dress with pearl and
gold necklace and earrings. She has the face and body
of a child, but I am aware she is older than I am. Only
once do we make eye contact. Our gaze spans centuries. We both nod our heads in acknowledgement of
mutual respect.

I stand up. The young couple flinches, drawing
closer to each other. I clear my throat for attention.

"Greetings friends. I am glad to see we all made our
way here safely. My name is Mr Caldwell, you know
me from the website forum as MrC. Now, each group
that decides to take this journey has a chance to nom-
inate a leader and you have chosen me. I would like to
thank you for giving me the privilege. It is my task to
ensure all of us keep safe, and to themselves, until the
allotted time. I will also be here to answer any questions you may have, although full guidance is beyond

my scope. For that you should refer to the custodians of the website, as I am merely one of you.

Rules are few and obvious. We do not attract attention to ourselves. If any of you are asked, we are part of a literary group here to discuss and explore the writing of the local area. I have some appropriate reading material, sent to me by the organisers, as cover for this purpose and which I shall hand out later. You should also have received a short email containing the names and synopses of works by local authors to be used should any particularly persistent individuals press you on the matter.

We order food and drink to our rooms. Choose a mid priced meal if you are unfamiliar with the choices. Feel free to use the billiard room, view a pay-per-view film and otherwise engage in such normal behaviours.

Finally, and absolutely, we *do not* feed tonight. If anyone *does* feed, and we will *all* know being in such close proximity, we are to disband immediately and that person or persons will be reported to the organisers for appropriate action to be taken. Those not responsible will have access to further guidance, and will have priority for the next available trip. Are there any questions?"

The girl from the young couple raises her hand.

"Has this been done before? I mean, organised like this?"

"Many times. Not here of course. For obvious reasons it must be a different location each time, to allay suspicion."

"And does everyone complete the journey?" The man from the couple spoke eagerly. I could tell he was hungry.

"As we discussed online, there is no pressure to be here or to remain here. Any one of us is free to leave at any moment before the meeting time." I look into his wet, fearful eyes. "After that time we are committed however, and nothing can stop us."

There was silence.

"Hey, Mr C! I got a question."

Vilmus had wandered over and was sitting on the back rest of the sofa to the annoyance of the older woman.

"Yes?"

"What, er. What was it you said earlier?"

"Which part exactly?"

"The bit after you said 'Greetings friends'."

Vilmus convulses in laughter, lost in his own private joke. We variously regard him with disdain or pity. He finally notices we are not joining in.

"Well screw you. That's enough talk. Talk makes me thirsty."

As Vilmus walks back to the bar to scrutinise the gin bottles, all but Emelia look at me.

"As for the meeting time, we gather in the foyer at 6.24 am and proceed from there. I think that is all I have to say as group leader, other than to wish you a good night."

***

It is 6.22 am and Vilmus is the last to join us in the lobby. He points past the reception desk towards the bar and says, "Refreshments, for the trip...", then disappears out of sight. We hear the clinking of glass bottles shortly after.

As I suspected, the young couple have fled. I have already sent a message to the organisers to let them know that it will be just the six of us completing the journey. We are all dressed the same as the night before, except for Emelia. She now wears an all black gown with a black veil that hangs to just below her shoulders.

Kelly's shift must have ended in the night, as it is a much older woman at the desk now. She barely looks at us. She reeks of disappointment. She has been doing this work for years and has no interest. It is a role she fills now, not a passion, or even a job. She doesn't look forward to retirement. She sees nothing ahead. She smells of roast chicken and peat. Ammonia curls. The same curls she has had for decades. She no longer cares. I wonder if she realises how alike we are? Would she be able to comprehend our journey? I feel she might have come with us, were she the same as us.

Vilmus comes back from the bar with a decanter of whisky in one hand. All of us, except Emelia, stare at him. He shrugs.

"It's a good one!"

I stand up.

"Now that we are all here, it is time. We have fasted, as is part of the ritual, and are now ready for the final part of our journey. There are only two things I have to say at this juncture..."

Vilmus removes the top of the decanter and takes a large swig. I continue, wearily.

"...firstly: the organisers wish us all well, and bless us on our journey. Secondly: this is the final opportunity for any of you to decide not to take the trip. You can leave now with no penalty or prejudice."

Nobody makes a move to leave. The German inspects and flattens his tie. I nod.

"Then it is time."

***

As the sliding doors open in response to the waft of the magazine I am carrying, the soft sting of light washes over my face. The sun is still below the horizon, yet I can already feel its flame. We gingerly step out into the car park. The landscape looks so alien in this light. In any light. Vilmus bounds over to a huge, angular car. A Mustang. He kisses the badge, stroking the bonnet.

"I'm gonna miss you baby. Not as much as you'll miss me eh? Heh-heh!"

Down the drive and on we walk.

The main road cuts a dead grey scar through the landscape, like a collapsed vein.

The mixed age couple suddenly start up an animated conversation about an almost forgotten holiday to Italy, the memory rekindled by the surroundings.

On we walk. Across the road and onto a stretch of sandy, grassy dunes so wide that I feel an enormous urge to stretch out both arms as if to touch the edges of the bay.

The dunes are quite tricky to navigate, as was expected. All of us slide and lose our balance at some point, except for tiny Emelia. Each of her steps is as precise as a wary cat. Vilmus downs whisky by the mouthful, stumbling and tumbling over the dunes by this point. A rather spectacular blind jump sees him land awkwardly, some six feet further down than he had expected. A hobble, a crunch of knitting bone and he laughs, arms and bottle raised to the paling sky, as if having defeated his final enemy.

On we walk.

The scrubby dunes give way to a flatter stretch of sand that is so soft it gulps at our ankles. The German sobs softly to himself, each step more difficult than the last, but nevertheless leading him to where he knows he must go.

Our eyes are hurting now as a rim of peach sky hugs the end of the sea. Our skin stings, as if under attack by hundreds of biting insects. Vilmus runs ahead, whooping in immaculate joy.

Here the soft sand becomes packed harder and darker, a flat plain wrinkled by tiny snake like pools of seawater. The shells and stones poking out of the sand cast monolithic shadows that ache to reach the mountains behind us.

On we walk.

We reach the edge of the water and stop. The sea lazily laps over stones and clumps of seaweed as we form a line to the sun. The German takes his shoes and socks off and stands in the water, letting it trickle over his toes.

Vilmus is behind us, dancing wildly in a circle, splashes of whisky sputting onto the sand.

I squint as the peach horizon turns to tangerine and the sea lights up. I clear my throat.

"We have seen more beauty than any man possibly should. More hell than any man could.

We have felt more joy than a life should allow. More agony than that we feel now.

We have known such great things as could..."

I look at my hands, tanning and drying before my eyes. Vilmus twists around himself, trying to fan out smoke that comes from all over him. The light bounces inside my eyeballs, scorching the inside of my skull. The couple hold each other tightly, burying their faces into each other's shoulders. The German falls to his knees in the water, muttering, "Sorry Rebekka," over and over in his own language.

"...such great things as could build a city. We have known such horrors as could destroy a country.

We have been as marvellous as we have been without breath. We will be... oh..."

The pain cuts me like a blade as my shrinking skin tightens across my shrivelling muscles, squashing them about my scorching bones. I feel I cannot say another word.

"...we will be nothing but dust in our moment of death."

It is Emelia, standing next to me. A tiny voice as delicate as a glass bell, as heavy as a flat, languorous ocean. Her features blacken before me, her eyes have already melted. I take her hand and turn to face the sun.

Vilmus makes a break for the mainland screaming, "I'm not ready!". But he won't make it to any shelter. It is too far. It was planned this way. Once we arrived at this spot, on this beach, we were all committed.

And just like words cut into wet sand, our ashes will be swept away with the tide, melting into the sea. It is time to stop being tired. Time to stop being hungry.

The sky's tangerine hue gives way to a raging red, pushing up from beyond the horizon. I haven't felt so awake, so aware in centuries. I understand now why Vilmus fled, but while his rush of realisation reminded him of past glories that kick-started his survival instinct, mine only makes me more resolute.

The burning rays of the sun peel me away like layers of old, dead paint. The light scars my eye sockets, carves its way through my ribcage and cooks my insides.

I finally feel warm again.

FAKE MARY

I first remembered her from last week, when she moved in a month ago.

No. No, that doesn't…

I'm stirring my latte. They put chocolate sprinkles on it again. I hate that. I did ask.

"Paul? Hey, how are you?"

It was Joni. Infectious smile and bouncing afro hair tied back.

"Hey there."

We hug. She looks either side of me, one eyebrow raised.

"Oh, yeah. She…"

She moved in a month ago. We met at Joni and Chris's gallery opening and came back to my place that same night.

I'd never done that before, even in my "wild" youth. I was no shark and I was always careful with relationships. But it all happened so quickly. I'd never met anyone like her. Funny. Genuinely funny, not put on. She'd have me in stitches in minutes, on any topic of conversation. And she was into modern art. Moved in the same circle of friends. It all just made sense.

That was a month ago.

But, I only met her... that doesn't make sense...

"Oh yeah. She left me."

"Oh no, you poor dear! Well, you look after yourself, OK?"

"Will do. Is Chris...?"

"Oh yeah, he's around, trying to hustle up some sales already. You know what he's like."

"Hi Joni!"

"Oh hi! Hey, have you two met before?"

"I think if we have the TV on *this* wall, then we can have bookcases either side, and use that space for a sideboard."

We were surrounded by boxes of all sizes, like a cardboard Grand Canyon.

My old place was a bachelor pad, not really big enough for two people to live in. So, eight months on, we're now renting a really nice apartment just on the edge of our salaries. Bit of a gamble, but the location is perfect for both our jobs, all our friends and favourite places. It's perfect really.

I grab her round the waist. She fakes pulling away, giggling, while I bring her to me and we share a passionate kiss.

"I'm glad your work let you have a few days off to sort this out. Would have been a nightmare otherwise."

"Yeah. New project doesn't start for a few weeks. The tech guys are still doing the planning, so I won't be on it full time until they've finished their bit."

"Yeah, you only work on the important bits, right?"

"Right! Now, talking of important projects, shall we see if the bed's still working?"

"Mmm. Might have been damaged in the move. Can't be too careful."

"Someone's got to test these things out…"
We smile.

That smile. So cheeky. I remember her…

"…his expression of anger in his paintings. Usually artists go overboard on black and red, wild brush strokes, like some angst-filled teenager, but he somehow manages to craft anger from a handful of pastel coloured geometric shapes. It looks too calm, like they're about to burst from the canvas in rage."

"A feeling of expectation."

"Yeah."

After Joni's introduction we had bumped into each other again while wandering round the gallery. We were upstairs where it was slightly quieter.

"You know Paul, I'm amazed we haven't met each other before now."

"Me too. How do you know Joni?"

"Uni. Different courses, but we met on the social scene." She eyeballs me. "We got pissed together."

We laugh. Her curly auburn hair bounces as she giggles.

"Yeah, I got that. So what do you do now?"

"I work for English Heritage. I'm their art expert. If someone applies for a building to be listed and it contains any frescos or mosaics or something, I'm the go-to girl."

"Wow. That's really cool."

She takes a step back. "That is *not* the response I usually get. It's typically somewhere between 'oh' and running for the door."

"Haha, no seriously, I'm interested."

She smiles at me. That's when I notice one corner of her mouth rises more than the other. And she has dimples. "So, seeing as we're going through the default questions now, what do *you* do?"

"Ah, nothing as interesting as you. I work for a tech company. Lead programmer, developing search algorithms to trawl image metadata for...", I realise I'm waving my arms and she's eyeballing me again. "Did I lose you?"

"Somewhere around 'Hello'."

I'm a father. I look into my daughter's beautiful blue eyes. We'll call her Mary I say. She agrees. I see a bath of blood.

No. Something isn't...

The taxi zooms off as she closes her turquoise shoulder bag and walks towards me from the kerb.

"Err…", I point after the disappearing cab. "That is going to your place without you?"

She smiles that slightly crooked smile again.

"Actually he's off to pick up three trannies from Soho."

I burst out laughing and steady myself on her shoulder. She puts a hand on my chest until I catch my breath again.

"Oh God, you're going to have to stop doing that you know, you'll kill me at this rate."

She's just smiling at me now. It makes me somewhat confused.

"Aren't you going to invite me in for a coffee?"

"I… ah, I just hope I have some."

"To be honest I don't really care."

She kisses me, wrapping her arms behind my neck.

I feel like I love her. Her… her name…

"I can't believe it's been two years already guys?"

"I know, amazing how time flies!"

Joni and Chris are sitting in our living room with their new baby boy. Mary is fascinated with him.

"Any chance of a baby brother for the little one?", asks Joni.

She laughs. "Oh God no. I'm not squeezing out another!"

"Yeah, I think one is plenty," I say. "Truth is, before I met you, I hadn't planned on having kids at all."

"Well, looks like you met the right person isn't it?"

I put my arm round her and kiss the side of her head. "Yep, looks like it."

"So…", says Chris, "…how's the work going? Or what you can tell us about it at any rate."

"Yeah, sorry. My work conversations are so boring. It's mostly "can't say", or "I could tell you but I'd have to kill you!"."

We all laugh. I sip my wine.

"But we're starting a new project soon. It will mean a few more hours, sorry love…", she fake punches me in the arm, "…but it's an important extension to our last project. It's going to cut search times down by weeks…"

Weeks. Weeks. It's been two years. It should have been weeks. Why are we only…?

85

"When? *When* will you be there? You missed her school play for Christ's-sake!"

"Oh my God, do you *have* to drag that up again? We had a milestone to hit, one of our seniors went off ill, we all had to pitch in to get it done. I already apolo-gised for this months ago! Do I have to set up a regular 're-apologise' calendar event or something?"

We're in our bedroom, both half undressed. We've been arguing for almost an hour, and I'm tired.

"Mary hardly sees you any more. *I* hardly see you any more. We haven't been intimate for months, you're always 'too tired'. I feel like you're a stranger we pass by in the street occasionally and say 'Hi' to 'cos we kind of recognise each other."

I rub my forehead. I can feel ripples of tiredness sloshing against my hand.

"Look. I'm sorry. Again! I'm sorry again. But I told you this was going to happen. This is how it works for us. It's not like you, where it's a steady stream of noth-ing until someone applies to have their bloody Vic-torian gazebo listed."

"Oh that's nice."

"But it's true! I've explained this before: work ramps up to milestones, then calms down again until the next one. It comes in waves. That's just how it works. And it doesn't help that our contractor has just accelerated the schedule. They want the bloody thing done in time for their US partners' system going live. We've lost three weeks! It's all…"

"All hands to the pumps? All hands on deck? Or did you mean another 'work hard' cliché in an industry that couldn't plan a four year old's birthday party? Oh, did I say a four year old's birthday party? Well that brings us nicely back round in a circle doesn't it?"

"I can't do anything about it. I can't take time off. I'm the lead programmer, I *have* to be there!"

"I can't sleep."

Mary is standing in the doorway, rubbing her eyes.

"Mary! Think of Mary!"

I know, I am. But which one?

"It's OK darling, come here. Daddy was just about to explain exactly what it is he has to do that's so important he can't come to your birthday party this year."

"You're not coming?" she starts to tear up.

"Oh Christ, that is totally unfair. Don't bring her into this like…"

"But it's her birthday party. I can't *not* bring her into this. So tell Mary, what exactly are you doing that's so bloody important?"

"Oh God! It's just the algorithm, we need to do some extra work on the heuristic analysis, it's not finding..."

"Mary! Think of Mary!"

I remember all the blood.

"What are you... who..."

She doesn't look angry any more. She looks like she's panicking.

"Tell us. Tell Mary!"

"Mary! Think of Mary!"

I am.

The memory arrives screaming to the front of my brain. I had buried it so far down, so deep, she hadn't found it.

It was the night of Joni and Chris's exhibition. I went alone. Mary had said she wasn't feeling well, and to apologise to them for not being there.

"Paul? Hey, how are you?"

It was Joni. Infectious smile and bouncing afro hair tied back.

"Hey there."

We hug. She looks either side of me, one eyebrow raised.

"Oh, yeah. She said she wasn't feeling well. Think she's coming down with the flu or something."

"Oh no, the poor dear! Well, you look after her, OK?"

"Will do…"

I had a nice time, a few drinks and went home alone in a taxi.

It was after 3am before I got home.

It was after 3am when I went into the bedroom to find an empty bed. I shrugged my booze filled shoulders and got undressed.

It was after 3am when I stumbled into the bathroom for a piss and found Mary in a bath of cold water and blood, wrists slashed open, glazed eyes just above the surface.

I pulled her head out of the water, held her to my chest, called her name.

Mary had said she wasn't feeling well, and to apologise to them for not being there. Except that was a lie for Joni and Chris. I had been so wrapped up in work, the start of the new project. She had forced me to take time off for the gallery opening (time that I would have to make up later), then said she didn't want to go, wanted a night in. I was pissed off at the bait and switch. She was pissed off I didn't want to spend time with her. I said I *did*, but at the gallery, which was the whole point of taking time off. And so on. We had a blazing row about it, a stupid argument. I hadn't seen how depressed she was, simply hadn't spotted it. She angrily said I should go on my own then. I angrily agreed, neither of us willing to give up our positions. I just hadn't spotted it.

I never met this girl at the gallery.

We never went home that night.

None of the past four years ever happened.

As I look at her, her face hardens. "Screw you," she says.

Her face, the room, the weeks, the years rush away from me like I'm falling backwards down a tunnel, until I'm hit by heat.

I'm stirring my latte. They put chocolate sprinkles on it again. I hate that. I did ask.

I look up and squint at the sun beating down on the small group of tables outside the café. A waiter delivers a filled croissant to the next table, apologising for the delay. A woman gets up near the window, slinging her bag over her shoulder, steadying herself. A child inside makes a face at me through the window, trying to get a response.

This is now. I'm back.

I call David on the emergency number. It's Sunday, but he picks up immediately.

"Clearance?"

"Turnkey-Action-Northwind four-five-four."

"Clear."

"Attempted psychic phishing. Just now. Arno's Café, Plymouth Street."

"Did they get anything?"

"Just fragments, nothing code specific."

"Eyes on?"

I look at the back of the girl slowly walking away along the pavement. Multicoloured flower summer dress, turquoise shoulder bag and ballet pumps. Trying to look casual, but staggering slightly from what must be a splitting headache. It's the curly auburn hair I recognise.

"Yeah, I see her."

"OK. Follow, do not engage, we'll be there in minutes."

The conversation ends.

I know it's not real, yet my whole body shudders at the implanted memory of Mary in the bathtub. A safety precaution, a hidden mental land-mine to be triggered should I, or any of us at the company, be targeted in a psychic espionage attempt. I can't wait to have that one buried again, have the gallery opening "honey pot" memory freshened up. Feel clean again.

I remember hugging her cold, wet body, crying until the emergency services turned up. It never happened. I shrug off the feeling of guilt, of sickness, and get up to follow the girl.

THE LAST VILLAIN

Better men than me have been laughed at for their theories, until they were proven right. And I *am* going to be proven right.

Thirty six years of work. One hundred and four journal submissions, all rejected. All funding applications denied. One BBC News science report, "balanced out" by the same establishment voices barring my work from publication, all framed and edited to make me look like a bumbling English fool with yet another crazy Cold Fusion theory. Even the University thinks I'm a crank now, and have told me not to name them in any further papers.

Bastards.

I want this to be a British invention, damn it! I'm sick of bloody American or Japanese labs contacting

me wanting to "team up", and of course they will need access to *all* my work. I'm not stupid. I've seen too many great ideas snapped up by other countries, credit taken by foreign groups. This has to be a British led, British created energy solution. Why is this so damned hard for people to accept?

Oh I know why. The "establishment" of course. They are either too invested in their own ideas or literally invested in the French ITER Nuclear Fusion project to want to allow any competing theory to flourish. It makes me sick.

So, that is why, in the end, I had to take matters into my own hands. As the saying goes: "If the mountain won't come to Mohammed…".

***

So this is my laboratory. It's actually a separate brick structure built at the back of my garden. Built from savings and from mortgaging the house for the first time in decades, it's large enough for what I require. I have sourced all the equipment and materials from universities and laboratories selling online. Some were harder to acquire, especially the reaction elements. One of those involved a special, private shipment out of Israel to avoid being tracked as a hazardous material. That cost a fortune.

Strictly speaking, the entire experiment I'm planning can only legally be carried out in an approved research space, far from any residential area. But, strictly speaking, it should have been carried out that way over twenty years ago, except the University wanted to partner with a German lab to do the actual experimentation while we focused purely on the calculations. I told them we did everything or nothing. So in a stunning display of their lack of any scientific endeavour (that I now know is deeply ingrained in their overly-conservative culture), they decided on "nothing".

In any case, I'm not some dumb American hick brewing up moonshine in his garage. I'm a Professor of Physics. I know laboratory and hazardous materials procedures. I know what I'm doing, and I'm not waiting any longer.

***

It has taken three years to complete the set-up for the experiment. Of course, with a team it could have been done in months, but that's humanity's lost time, not mine. I have triple-checked every detail, especially the software side, which is not my particular forté. Unknown to them, the University lab staff and my students have been very helpful in answering my specific queries, carefully framed as general questions of interest.

It all works too. I have done the calibration tests. Some tweaks were required, but I wasn't off by much. I am very pleased with how well it came together. From the outside it looks like a giant metal beach ball with tubes and wires connected to computers and pumps. It looks a mess to be frank, but it doesn't have to be beautiful to work.

Of course, when I *do* get results they won't accept them because it's not a "proper" laboratory setting. But at least when I get my preliminary data, showing more energy in than out, they will take my theory more seriously. I will get funding, and set up a state-of-the-art British lab to take it further. Until then, my "science shed" will have to do.

I triple-check the material volumes and weights, power supply input, sensors, and prepare for experiment 01.

***

Oh Joy! The joy of being right! In fact I was even more right than I had anticipated. The reaction sustained itself for far longer than I had thought it would, some 4.36 seconds. Current experimental LENR energy outputs are one-time reactions measured in the milliseconds. Compared to those, this is a lifetime!

Energy in: 914W. Energy out 16,742W. Over eighteen times more energy out than in! Even ITER are only aiming for ten times the output and that's in a massive reactor that's costing ten billion to build. My reaction happens at 282.6 Kelvin. You could have it running on your desk!

Almost forty years waiting to know I was right. I cried. I admit I cried. I am not ashamed. Tears of relief... no, tears of affirmation. I opened a vintage whisky I was given as my 50th birthday present and had a large glass as I paced the living room in excitement. Yes, excitement. THIS was science. This was what those people (I won't deign to call them actual scientists) at the University had given up experiencing thanks to their own regretful lack of vision. When you run a university like a business, you become risk-averse. Any outcome that can't be predicted doesn't fit their business project plans. But most theoretical physics' outcomes can't be predicted! Yes, the calculations show what *should* happen, but sometimes you don't know what you'll find. That's what science is about: discovery and risk. Even a negative result can open up a huge new branch of investigation. But for them, a negative result equals a waste of money. They didn't get their planned outcome, so further funding denied. Idiots. Utter idiots.

***

On repeating the experiment with the exact same circumstances I saw virtually the exact same results. Repeatable. Measurable. Curious about the self-sustaining nature of the reaction, I did some branching experiments with modifications to power input and material amounts, and discovered... something wonderful. A self-sustaining reaction! I only have to keep topping up a tiny amount of material every few hours for a continuous energy output. It is only twelve times the energy output, compared to the initial experiments, but this is unprecedented.

This is it. I have created the future of clean energy production for humanity. It's in a brick hut in the back of my garden. Hah! That's the British way though isn't it? Mucking through. Unlikely discoveries in unlikelier places, often by accident. Except this was no accident. I had the science behind me to know I was right. By God I was right!

Time to stop feeding material in, wait for the reaction to cease and then time to analyse the data. This is going to be one hell of a paper. It's going to blast those establishment figures off their pedestals! I can't wait.

***

Three days after discontinuing feeding the material, the reaction is still ongoing. It took me some time to work out how that was possible, until I noticed a small puddle of water underneath the sphere. Condensation had been dripping off it onto the floor. I had been so wrapped up in calculations of the reaction itself I hadn't noticed the temperature readings from inside the walls of the sphere. While the reaction was carrying on at around 284 Kelvin, the actual internal temperature of the sphere was now 261 Kelvin and dropping. I took a thermometer to the outside of the reaction chamber and it's just above freezing point.

It seems the reaction is highly endothermic. Not finding any more material to use in the sealed vacuum of the chamber, it has started to draw in energy through the walls of the chamber in order to sustain itself. In layman's terms, it's hungry and wants to eat.

I calculate that cooling the chamber to as close to absolute zero as possible should stop the reaction; starve it of energy. I set about purchasing the materials to allow me to do so, but they will take some days to arrive. A week to assemble safely. No, I will have to take some time from work. This has to be done quickly.

But no need for undue panic. This is just an unforeseen factor. Once the cooling system is in place and working I will have full control over the reaction again and can continue my experiments.

This is science. Sometimes things happen that you don't expect. That's what makes it so exciting!

***

The second hand cooling system I procured has proven to be temperamental and inefficient. I can barely get it consistently down to 176 Kelvin for five hours before it develops some problem. I'm certain I have set it up correctly. Just my luck some Northern university had a piece of crap machine they were willing to dump on an unsuspecting scientist. I have set about releasing some finances to find a more modern replacement. I will have to buy new.

As it is, the reaction is still ongoing with some mildly concerning developments. In the process of fitting the cooling system, I removed the glass tubes used to feed in the reaction materials, only to discover the parts which were inside the chamber had gone. Completely eaten away, presumably subsumed by the reaction and used to power it. The chamber itself is 18mm thick steel. The tubes had only 11mm left beyond the outer seal. I have to assume therefore, that the inside wall of the chamber itself has been eaten away in a similar manner and is now similarly only 11mm thick.

With the finances I am releasing for the new cooling system, I will also need to acquire a larger containment chamber. Nothing fancy, just a big thick metal box to surround the sphere in the unlikely event that it would be breached. If that happened, there would be a minor implosion and the reaction would then be able to access the heat and matter outside.

This is all just as a precaution of course. I have to get the reaction stable, or stopped, controllable at the very least, to be able to present it. In its current state there would be panic, the opposite of the intelligent thought that these so-called scientists are supposed to possess. But they are the gatekeepers. For them, and for them only, I need to overcome this setback.

***

The new chamber and cooling system arrived. The outer chamber took some pulled muscles and a great deal of sweat to put together. I was already in a bad mood because I had to almost physically remove the delivery men from the front hall, they were so adamant on "installing" it for me. I saw them, looking around the front of my house, puzzled. Well it's my business and none of theirs! Their job is to drive a truck and drop off boxes. Leave the science to me thank you.

There was a problem however. The cooling system was so different to the old one it took far longer than intended to set it up. It was early morning by then, I had barely eaten, hardly had anything to drink. The sphere had been in the new chamber without any cooling for hours, so I had to hurry. I was hurrying. It was stupid. A stupid mistake. I had reconnected the air pumps to the new chamber, but hadn't turned them on. I was so fixated on getting the bloody *cooling* system working, I clean forgot.

So instead of simply disintegrating inside a new safe vacuum, the sphere imploded violently. So, there was now a large chunk of metal to feed the reaction, not to mention nearly 150 cubic litres of warm air inside the chamber that hadn't been pumped out.

I was furious with myself. I was cursing aloud, almost crying in frustration. But I wasn't defeated. Eventually I did set up the cooler and turn on the pump. It was finally done.

However I had no sensors wired up to this new chamber. Didn't have time to fit them all. I was blind.

Those bastards at the journals, at the University! Putting me through all this just to prove their ignorance. This is my experiment and I am going to complete it. I am going to show them!

***

I can no longer enter the laboratory. Internal temperature has dropped to 206 Kelvin and the computers keep crashing as moisture freezes inside them. I briefly considered the logistics of removing all the equipment from inside, and turning the whole room itself into a sealed vacuum chamber. I could have done it if I had got an extension to the mortgage on the house, but the bank wouldn't allow it, wanted to ask too many questions. "Why?", they kept asking, like an ignorant child with only the vaguest understanding of how the universe works. In the end I walked out mid-conversation. They didn't deserve my time.

So, instead, thanks to the ignorance of others, this is the situation we are in.

My suitcase is packed. No point taking much with me. I stand in the kitchen at the back of the house, looking out at the laboratory as I drink one final cup of tea. I think of all the, "If only"s. If only they had listened to me all those years ago. If only they had set up a lab to work on this back then. We could have done this in properly controlled conditions, not forced, like some beggar, to pinch old, not-fit-for-purpose equipment and cobble it together in a brick shed. This was the scientific discovery of the century. They wanted me scrabbling round in the dirt to prove myself right. Well, they got it. This is my legacy. This is what they have now, and it's all on them.

As I stand there, the window in the centre of the facing wall of the lab cracks.

Time to go.

***

The bar in Chiang Mai is half full. A mix of local Thais and tourists. There is no chatter. Everybody is focused on the flat screen TV hanging on the wall, listening to the news report.

"...four nuclear bombs will be detonated simultaneously one mile from the centre of the reaction sphere. They have to be detonated at this distance because if they were to fly any closer to the centre they would disintegrate. Turned harmlessly to dust. Scientists hope that this will be enough to 'overcharge' the reaction and bring it to a halt, even though they are still not entirely sure of the processes going on inside the sphere.

The sphere itself is now sixty miles wide stretching from Gloucester in the West to Luton in the East, from Leamington Spa in the North to Basingstoke in the South. It continues to expand by almost a kilometre per day, eating up any matter it comes into contact with. There is also a 'rip-tide zone' of around four miles around the sphere where the air in the atmosphere is being sucked towards it.

It is because of this constant expansion that the strike has to be done now. Scientists have determined that the sphere will soon be too large for even the fastest rocket to carry a warhead large enough, close enough to the centre of the reaction to have any effect.

Evacuation programmes from the UK to mainland Europe have been ongoing for weeks and have been accelerated in anticipation of the strike."

"But not everyone agrees this is the right course of action do they?"

"No, in fact some experts say that the nuclear explosion itself could *feed* the reaction, triggering a massive expansion of the sphere. They say the reaction *has* to be self-limiting, that it's impossible for it to expand forever. For their part, the experts on the side of the nuclear strike say that that's what *they* thought when the reaction sphere reached the boundaries of Oxford. But now they say this is the best chance we have to do anything, as doing nothing simply isn't an option."

"It could have been the saving of humanity you know."

The young American couple are startled by the voice behind them. They turn to see an old English man sitting in the corner. He is wearing a bright floral shirt, linen shorts and flip-flops. Sunglasses hang round his neck by a chain as he sips a cold drink.

"I'm sorry?"

"The arrogance of ignorance. They would rather watch a monthly dollop of cash safely land in their bank accounts than care about the future. Now they have condemned it."

The couple look at each other, confused.

"What, the scientists trying to stop this? They're trying to save the world! They don't care about money."

The Englishman closes his eyes and chuckles, enjoying some private joke.

The male tourist is visibly angered by this.

"You're laughing? You think this is funny? This thing could destroy the planet. Humanity is at the brink of extinction, man!"

"Maybe I don't care. Maybe I never did. Maybe this planet of fools needs to be sunk so a better one can rise in its place."

The couple don't know what to say.

The man finishes his drink, stands up and picks a straw hat off the table before putting it on his head. For the first time since he entered the bar, he looks at the TV.

"They won't stop it you know."

"How do you know?" asks the girl.

"Because it's my legacy to show people their ignorance. If that means destroying them all? So be it."

And with that, the man walks out into the sunshine, as the launch countdown begins.

LORD OF SHADOW

"But ... shadows must be something. They can't be nothing?"

Mummy gives Dad a funny look. She's shaking again. Things are silent for a bit so I scrape my knife across the plate through the beans' sauce trying to make rows of straight lines like a farmer's field. I imagine planting baked beans and growing rows and rows of baked bean trees that I'd harvest once a year and sell to Tesco. Eventually Dad speaks.

"Shadows are nothing Simon. They are just... places where the light isn't. Because light is bright the shadows are dark. They aren't a 'thing'."

Scrape. Scrape. Scrape.

"Then why is Mummy afraid of them? You can't be afraid of nothing?"

Mummy gets up quickly, bumping the dinner table making the plates and knives and forks jump. She walks to the sink. She just stands there shaking while Dad looks at her back.

"People are afraid of different things... silly things... post boxes!", he says, turning to look at me with a strange wide grin on his face. "I remember reading about this man who was terrified of red post boxes. Couldn't go near them. Completely silly."

He looks at me like one of those crossword puzzles he can't get. I stare back down at my plate. Scrape. Scrape. George starts hammering his yellow plastic spoon onto his high chair table. It's annoying but Dad doesn't stop him.

"But even if it's nothing, the fear of it is real. Isn't it Dad?" When I look up he's staring at Mummy's back again.

"Yes Simon. That's real."

George starts kicking his legs and Dad fusses with his food.

I can't tell them about the shadows, they wouldn't believe me. If they even listened.

***

We are on the hills behind our house and I'm trying to kick my ball straight, but it keeps going off to the side. Mummy made me dress up warm because it's cold, even though the sun is out.

The ball goes to the left this time under some bushes. I run and pick it up then look back down the hill. I like it up here. The houses are like little cardboard boxes, in straight and curvy rows as they head towards town. They are all lit up with the sun, the windows shining, hurting my eyes, apart from the Brightmans at number twelve who had, "an expensive waste of money put in when they got their windows done", according to Dad.

Dad is halfway between me and the cardboard houses. He tucks in George's tiny clothes as he squirms in the push-chair and talks to him in his silly voice. The same one he uses to talk to cats.

Dad calls me on because they are heading back to the house then talks to George again. He is always talking to George. So is Mummy. But she's not here this time, she wanted a lie down.

"Dad, watch this!"

I'm going to kick this one straight and show him I can do it. I put the ball down on the grass and try to stop it rolling down the hill.

"Dad!"

George is kicking his legs and Dad tries to distract him.

"Dad, look!"

He doesn't look and calls me to hurry up. I suddenly don't care any more and let the ball roll down the hill, bouncing over clumps of grass as it tries to get to the house before Dad and George.

Something seems funny today. I can feel the sun on my face, but it doesn't tingle me as it usually does. I feel cold even with my coat on. As I'm standing there the sun goes down behind the hill. The windows stop shining at me and the grass around me gets darker and darker. All the houses are starting to fade into the same colour as the shadows smother them.

Dad calls me again to come back to the house, but I feel happy here. I feel warm now. I don't need my coat on. I could take it off and run around in my t-shirt all evening until it went dark and I felt tired. But I know they won't let me. So I stomp all the way down the hill to pick up the ball, stomp up the back garden path, stomp through the kitchen and drop it in the hallway. They don't even notice.

***

Mummy is talking to George in his room as I make the toothpaste froth in my mouth. I do a big horse grin until I start to dribble a bit then spit it out. Then I watch the curling water suck it down the plughole.

I'm bouncing around in my bed when Mummy eventually comes through and stops me.

"Sleep tight Simon." She kisses my forehead and looks at me like Dad did earlier before turning off the light and closing the door.

I hear George screaming and banging the bars of his cot. Then Mummy's voice. And after ages he settles and Mummy goes to her and Dad's room. I hear the murmurs of them talking but can never make out what they are saying. I pull the duvet up to my throat and stare up at the ceiling. It's only a few minutes before the shadows start moving. They creep out from the corners of the room, slowly at first, like they don't want me to see them. But then I get all tingly and they start swaying back and forth on the walls or swirling around the ceiling, making me dizzy. I was afraid of them at first but they never hurt me and I look forward to them now because I feel warm and nice. I smile at them and they dance for me.

I sit up in bed and watch the criss-cross window shadow spin across my duvet. I put out my arm and turn my fingers around, making it go faster and faster and faster until it breaks apart into short wiggling lines that fly into the corners. I giggle then stop myself in case Mummy and Dad hear me. Sounds like they did as their bedroom door opens and Mummy, I think, comes out. I quickly lie down and stay totally still. The shadows huddle the other side of my bed. But she goes straight into George's room and stays there for a bit before coming back out and into their room again. I suddenly feel angry. This happens all the time. Any noise they hear and it's straight into George's room to check on him. They never check on me. It's not like I scream and shout or get upset like George does, but I miss them worrying about me. They don't seem to care any more.

I feel my right arm is suddenly warm and see a shadow covering it. I smile. The only things that care about me now are the shadows, and they are the only things I care about too.

Sliding out of bed I tip-toe out onto the landing. It's so quiet I can hear the small night light on the wall buzzing. I go into George's room. He's asleep, breathing through a snotty nose and kicking his foot. Mummy has left his toy light on above the cot as always. I turn it off leaving the moon to light the room through the open curtains. I know how the side of the cot slides down and do it without making a sound. As I lift him out and put him on the floor on his belly he wakes up and looks at me. He looks angry. I don't care, I'm the one who's angry. I'm sick of him. Why do they always fuss over him? Why can't Mummy talk to me in bed like she used to? I stand up and I'm shaking. I hate George. Why can't he just go? I feel like crying and I don't know why.

Then I feel a tingle, as if the sun is on my face. I look down and the shadows are wrapped around my arms. And then they move towards George. The shadow of a cot bar wraps itself round his ankle and he starts shaking oddly. He just stares at me, trembling.

"Stop looking at me." I hadn't meant to speak out loud.

115

The cot bar shadows move again and curl around his neck. His eyes are wide now and he's still shaking, still looking right at me.

"Stop it!" I start crying. "Stop doing that."

He's shaking really badly now. The shadow is tight round his neck. His hands start coming off the floor and banging down on it. His head slowly tilts back and he spits a bit. His eyes roll down to stare at me again.

"Stop it! Just go away and stop it!" I scream, and the shadows drag him across the floor, his little hands beating on the carpet. His legs disappear into the side of the cupboard, then his chest and arms until all that's left is a bit of his face, now completely still, like a broken bright doll. Then he's gone.

Mummy comes into the room first. I'm still crying and staring at the side of the cupboard. She asks me what I'm doing out of bed then turns the light on. The shadows quickly leave. I feel cold. Then she says, "Where's George?". Then she asks me where he is. I just sob. She is moving furniture when Dad comes in wondering what's going on. Tears are running down her face as she says George has gone. They both look at me and Mummy gets onto her knees, grabs my shoulders and shakes me. She asks over and over again where is George, what have I done with him.

"I haven't done anything." I say "The shadows took him."

***

"What can the police do?" screams Mummy. I can only hear parts of what they say as I sit at my desk by my bed. It's morning now. From the window I can see the house makes a big flat shadow going out the back garden and up the hill.

"...only way then." says Dad. "If they can't help then (mumble). Do you still have the number?" I think Mummy starts crying again.

I should have gone to school today and Dad should have gone to work too. But he's downstairs and I've been told to stay in my room, so I decide to do a drawing of the house for them. I like doing drawings, but they don't look at them any more. Maybe they will now George has gone. As I'm doing the sky they answer the door to someone.

"Thank you for coming so quickly. We didn't know what else..." A man mutters something in a really low voice – not Dad – and they let him in. He feels big, the shadows downstairs are squeezed around him. I hear them making tea but not what they are saying. It must be the police about George going missing but Mummy's right, I don't know what they could do either.

I finish the house by doing a puff of smoke coming out of the chimney. Dad will see the funny side of that 'cos we have gas. I drew the flowers in the front garden for Mummy. I always used to help her water them.

I hear more bits of what they are saying as I come down the stairs. The sun at the front of the house makes funny long door shadows across the carpet and down the hall to the kitchen where I see Dad sitting and the back of a man in a suit.

"I don't pretend to understand at all..." Dad sees me at the front door and Mummy looks round the large shoulder of the suit man.

"Simon," Dad smiles oddly. "We've got... there's someone here to see you."

"I did a drawing of our house..." I walk towards them.

"That's... lovely."

"...with the flowers I helped Mummy water and the chimney." I hold it out in front of me as I reach the doorway and smile.

"Simon."

Neither of them looks at me much. I had almost forgotten about the suit man until I hear a zip go. I pull the picture to my chest. The man has a small black square bag in his hands and is pulling a zip all the way around it. He has lots of wrinkles. They look like he's had them all his life and go all across his face.

"Hello there Simon." He smiles and all the wrinkles smile.

Something metal clinks in the bag and Mummy puts her hand up to her mouth.

"I've done a picture for Mummy and Dad." I say to make sure he knows it's not for him.

"That's very good. Now Simon, my name is Matthew. I've been talking to your parents..."

"I don't know where George has gone." I try not to shout.

"That's all right, I know you don't. You can't possibly know. But that's really all right." The sound of his deep voice makes me sleepy. I see something silver and round come out of his bag.

"Now Simon, he's a friend of ours..." Dad gives me that odd smile again and I hear the edges of my picture crunch in my hands. The silver thing goes click and I see some shiny white stuff inside some glass. I hear the shadows screaming at me.

"Simon", says the suit man, "your Mummy, Daddy and I have agreed that we all need some time apart right now. We need to find your little brother George and we can't do that while you're here. It's too danger-ous for you."

Faster than I notice he's suddenly standing up and I back down the hall. My breath is heavy through my nose and I crunch up the drawing even more.

"I drew them a house!"

"I can't do this..." Mummy shakes her head and walks backwards from Dad.

My legs start to tremble and I knock something on the hall table with my elbow that clatters. The suit man fills the doorway.

"It's all right Simon. We've agreed it's for the best."

"NO!" I jump as my back touches the front door. I turn and try the handle. It's locked. The key is always in the lock, but it's not there. I crouch down and start crying as he comes towards me. I feel a bit sicky.

"Don't be afraid, it's all right..."

I wish he'd stop saying that. It's not. I did a drawing for Mummy and Dad and they didn't look at it and now they're saying this man can take me away. Noth-ing is all right. They don't care. They just pretend to, when all they care about is George. Why do they still care about him? He isn't even here now. I wish they all weren't here.

I suddenly feel warm, as if the sun was on me, and my face tingles. I drop the picture and stand up. The suit man says something but I can't make it out, it's all watery mumbles. The thin glass window of the door is right behind me and my shadow is in front of me. The suit man has the silver thing in front of him and starts to bend down.

"Go away," I say.

And he does. All his wrinkles freeze and my shadow covers him from head to toe and then he's gone into the floor.

"Oh God!" Dad gets up, knocking the chair over. Mummy turns round and looks all the way down the hall.

"Where...?"

"Just... Helen, just go." Dad pushes her towards the back door, trying to stand between me and her. I start to walk down the hall, dragging the shadows with me.

"Why don't you want me here Mummy? George has gone now, why don't you want me?" Mummy screams, she's making a lot of noise with the keys in the lock.

"It's not that we don't... Helen come on... the man, he... he just" Dad's arms wave around.

The door opens. Mummy screams Dad's name and they almost fall out into the garden. I close my eyes and can feel the shadows hugging me from inside. I don't care that Mummy and Dad don't want me now, the shadows saved me from that man, the shadows want me. Mummy cries out and I open my eyes. I walk through the kitchen and out the back door.

They are running up the hill now, the back gate shaking angrily as it bounces closed. But they can't run. My arms tingle and I lift them up, pushing the house shadow up the hill behind them. Dad screams something at Mummy, but I make the chimney shadow trip her up. She rolls onto her back. Her eyes are wide and she tries to scream but makes no sound as she goes black and flat and disappears into the grass. Dad's crying, "No, no..." as he runs away, but the tree shadow catches up with him. The branch shadows lift him into the air by his ankle, before covering him and cutting him into shivering black ribbons.

It's finally quiet.

No suit man. No George. No Mummy and Dad. Just me and the shadows.

MAKING GODS

I stared at the photo and the two black, hollow eyes seemed to burrow into the space beyond. Susan moved suddenly and I jumped, shifting my eyes from the image and back to her. The archaeology department's current expedition near Cobá had uncovered some brand new Mayan artefacts from a sink hole, including some exquisite carvings. Mike, our intrepid Aussie explorer, had immediately emailed photos to linguistics, and Susan was in her element.

"See this section here is identical to the passage..." she rummaged around her desk as files dropped to the floor and scurried under bookshelves, "...here! The Copan carving found sixteen years ago."

She showed me the two images side-by-side as she brushed her coppery hair behind her ear. The older find had weathered and the pictograms were softer, like ink spreading across a wet page. The new carving had been buried for centuries and was superbly preserved.

"This first one is the famous Votan or 'Old Black God' invocation found by Dressler and Harman in late 1990. The stone was incomplete, but what was there was translated. The missing piece was never found."

She stared at the old picture, dejected. She was always so open with her feelings. I could always tell she was never happy with him.

Her face suddenly brightened. "But now this new carving contains almost the full invocation *and* fills in the missing gaps. We will finally have a complete Mayan invocation! Can you imagine it?" She smiled at me and all my worries melted away. She slid round behind her desk with a willowy elegance and started work almost immediately. When she was passionate about something, there was nothing else in the world to care about.

I was so glad to see her like this again. For the last year or so she just hadn't been her lively self. She was purely functional. A free spirit caged. No-one had said anything of course, but we were all glad when she left him. I was glad when she left him.

"I've... ah... got to go now Sue."

"OK. '...completeness to have knowledge of...', '...to be aware of the end', '...judgement...'".

I hesitated to interrupt, but it was too good an opportunity. I had been waiting some time to ask after all.

"Ah... look. There's a nice new, er, Greek place opened up on Portland Street. I don't know if... I mean obviously you're busy now, but maybe the weekend sometime, if you'd like... um, eat..."

"I'd love to."

Her reply caught me slightly off guard, as I had been staring anywhere but her face to make it easier to speak. When I looked at her she was posed with one hand in the air holding some papers and just smiling at me.

"OK, well I'll, er, call you later to sort a time... you know, around your work here, and..."

"OK. Take care David."

***

Some days later I found her at her desk, books surrounding her like worshippers at an altar. She had been struggling with part of the translation. It could have several meanings depending on the interpretation and she had been busy comparing it with other known work. Sumerian was my personal speciality, but I volunteered to lend a hand to help out, and I relished the chance to talk with her.

"See... this passage refers to the priest, the one who calls to the God to imbue them with its power. But it says something to the effect of, 'the one who *cannot* see shall guide/lead/whatever', which doesn't make sense. The priests are the ones who can see 'above all'. That's their purpose."

I was definitely intrigued.

"Well what else does the text say about sight or looking?"

"Part of the originally translated passage forms a warning for those casting the invocation. It says, 'To the unseeing, Votan grants his power. To the seeing, Votan takes their life.'"

I picked up the emailed photo and looked at the image of the God. It was a giant, square figure with circles for eyes, none of the elaborate decorative effects usually found on Mayan carvings, apart from the tiniest of human figures standing in the palm of its hand.

"Well, in the Christian Bible, God says 'You cannot see My face, for no man can see Me and live!'. Basically, us little fleshy animals can't survive looking in the eyes of a God, it's too much for us to take in. Maybe a similar belief..."

"Oh my God." Sue sat down. "No pun intended by the way."

"None taken," I smiled.

She took her glasses off and started to fold them slowly. This was her "deduction" habit. I loved watching her do this.

"There have been skulls found in some sites – full ritual burials of priests – with scrape marks inside the orbits. They'd had their eyes gouged out."

We looked at each other with grim mutual comprehension.

"Well, on that rather gruesome note, um... Greek? Saturday?"

Sue had been deep in thought, but now looked up, her eyes bright. "Yes, is about 11am OK? The time difference you see – Mike is sending me some more images so I'll be up late..." she tilted her head to the other side "...early." She giggled.

"Sure."

I left her poring over old texts as I wondered what I had to wear that didn't make me look like a slightly overweight linguist in my mid-forties.

***

Just before nine am on Saturday I got a phone call from her, asking me to come over to her apartment. She was very excited, and all she would say was, "I've finished it!"

She didn't live far from the Greek place, so we wouldn't have far to walk later. I was going to pay anyway of course, but if she had finished translating the full passage then dessert was going to be my treat too. Her place was pretty much as I had imagined. The communal stairs had little cactus plants on each landing and her apartment smelt a joyful mix of flowers and marshmallows. She was almost bouncing up and down with glee as she explained her translation methods, why she'd used certain words and phrases, how the remaining text had helped her decipher three previously untranslated glyphs, and told me how it all confirmed her initial theory of the passage.

She sat back on the edge of her desk and started to read the invocation out loud. How someone could do this to me I don't know. I was Mr Boring and always had been. I knew this. My ex-wife told me many times. But there I was, listening to Sue and I had never felt so vibrant. Her vitality made me feel alive by proxy and had made me stop handing in my resignation for months. And as she sat there, the morning sunlight making her hair glow orange around her face I nearly cried with happiness as I realised I was in love.

She finished reading and looked at me, swinging her legs and grinning like a happy child.

"Susan, I..."

Then her face stopped glowing. The beams of light crossing the walls from the blinds dissolved and the warmth left the room. A note played. A note so deep my guts liquefied. It reverberated through the walls and the floor. The dust floating in the air vibrated with it and I felt sick like I was falling. I grabbed her by the arm and pulled her towards me as the huge black hand scooped through the front of the apartment buildings, dragging windows, curtains and bookcases with it.

Another note. My chest compressed and my heart felt like it was going to be squeezed dry. I managed to force out the word, "Run!", and we fled. Down past the cacti and into the front lobby. Through the frosted glass of the front door all we could see was flame and debris falling to the floor. "The alley!", Sue screamed and pulled me out the back.

Hurtling out of the alley we collided with somebody running and they fell hard onto the pavement. While I tried to stammer an apology they rolled over, looked past our heads into the sky, gasped and exploded into flames. Within a second they were nothing more than a blackened skeleton and flecks of charcoal rising into the air. Sue screamed. Then we both saw the world slowly ending in front of us. A dark red sky hung over the city, casting nightmarish shadows across our view. People were running, falling, crying, looking up at the impossible being towering over the apartments behind us, then bursting into fire. Cars collided as the people inside erupted, sparks billowing out slit-opened windows.

Only the crashing sound of Sue's apartment block collapsing broke us out of our reverie. Another note. Paving slabs shifted out of alignment and windows fell from their frames. I dragged her between the crashed cars, the air starting to taste like ash. I feebly shouted, "Don't look at it's eyes!", while feeling my own eyes being sucked back into their sockets, some magnetic force almost unbearably compelling me to look.

We ran past a fast food place as the families sitting at the window vaporised in swift succession, leaving inky smears on the glass. Sue was crying now, saying it was all her fault, I told her it wasn't. How could she have known? How could anyone have known?

An explosion. I chanced a glance back at ground level and saw a waterfall of dust and brick as a giant black square foot punched through two storeys of a building. Screams and fire erupted wherever this thing touched. The city behind us was aflame.

I pulled her towards the park. The underground was just the other side. If we could get down there we would be safe. We *might* be safe. Hell, I didn't have a clue.

Sue started to resist me pulling her, but I said, "We can make it." As we passed the pond, Sue stopped.

"I can't. I can't..." she sobbed.

I grabbed her by the shoulders. "Look, we get into the underground. It might not be able to get us there."

"But it's after us isn't it? It's after me. It won't stop until it gets me... I'm its guide. I called it."

"But if we hide from it, stop it getting to you then it might go... away, somewhere... might give up, I don't know, we've got to try!"

"I know how to stop it."

Sue had stopped crying now and I could feel the heat increasing on one side of my face. Crash – another footstep. Boom – another lung-crushing note.

"No. Sue. Don't. You can't... I..."

Boom. The note pushed my shoulders down into my chest as I felt my eyes bulge. The trees erupted into flames and charred birds fluttered out of the sky like impossibly dark leaves.

Sue looked at me forlornly.

"It's calling me. Can't you hear it? It needs me to guide it, and if I'm not here..."

Crash. The footstep cracked the pathway under our feet as the pond started to boil.

"... then neither is it."

"Please, Sue, I..."

Then she smiled again and all my worries melted away. She leant over and kissed me. A first kiss. A last kiss.

"It's OK."

It was crouching down, its giant hand resting close by us, palm upwards. All I could taste was ash.

I took her hand, and as she turned to face it, I looked away. There was the faintest sound, like a sudden intake of breath, then dark flakes of her flowed around me. I wasn't sure what to do, so I held onto her hand until the sky turned blue again.

THE COLOURS OF JUPITER

"Awake child, awake. My life is just beginning and you will never see yours in the same way again. Open your eyes and awake."

I open my eyes and see all the colours of Jupiter flowing through time.

***

"Cheryl Hawkins. ID 170045-D."

The door beeps its confirmation and glides open.

Inside the golden-orange chamber Mackie is tapping up the coordinates for the next test cycle as I hand my data to Emit. As he checks my work I stare through the thick glass, through the stellar dust, to the giant silver sphere hanging like a ridiculous bauble

between our ship and Jupiter. A caged black hole. A giant electromagnetic trap to house our experiment. I've had nightmares where I reach out through the glass, impossibly touching it, and the shell crumples like foil. Microseconds later my arm is scoured off...

"The turning point in human history Cheryl, and you can't stop thinking it looks like a kid's toy, can you?"

"I didn't think I was in the habit of designing children's playthings Emit."

He snorts a laugh, "We're all playthings Cheryl, pulled by invisible strings, we just can't see it."

Ignoring him I take my seat and confirm Mackie's beam trajectories. I look over my shoulder and see Petter is outside the security door shouting at it. All this technology and we still can't get voice recognition software that understands his thick Ukrainian accent. Forcing himself through the first available narrow opening, he apologises for his lateness. Apparently the suction on toilet four wasn't working properly. We all tell him to spare us the details.

"Tango-Foxtrot Two to Omega Control. Confirm all matter inputs minimal. Awaiting cycle. Over." The radio blips.

Emit replies, "This is Omega Control, received. 88% power Cycle begins in T-minus fifteen minutes, 18 seconds."

Petter circles his workstation like a frustrated dog that's lost the scent, before seemingly hitting a random button. My workflow is a perfect branching tree of possibilities, each branch opening or closing based on parameters reached, conditions established. Petter appears to get everything done purely by accident. Superb engineer. Utterly infuriating to work with.

Branch twenty-three – beam coordinates entered and accepted by generators. Matter inputs stable and still charging.

I see Emit gazing at the real-time data display of the thousands of sensors in the Temporal Interference Chamber surrounding the singularity. Such a brilliant man, but I do wonder if the protracted development of the project has affected his investment in it. When he first sought me out to design the sphere he had it planned to completion, every detail, every day up until the experiment was complete. But with each passing year he's seemed to care less for the details, allowing the Council full control over the project management. Now he barely enters into any technical discussions, leaving it entirely to the rest of the team. He spends hours staring at all the plans and data, as if looking for some missing piece. Of course it's liberating that our lead scientist is entrusting so much of the running of this project to us. All our futures are assured whatever the outcome and we all owe him a lot, particularly me. But his lack of guidance at this critical phase is disconcerting. It's like he's a passenger.

Branch twenty-four – matter input starts at T-minus fifteen minutes.

I look out the window at the sphere. I think it's going to be another routine test cycle.

***

"Thing is..." Mackie takes the opportunity between two words to fill himself with another fork of spaghetti, "...if the first full power test does confirm time is non-linear..."

"There is little chance it's going to do that. Only with full power plus the correct beam energy signatures are we potentially going to see any interference patterns. Finding the correct ones could take years, decades even."

My interjection doesn't put him off.

"... then what does that actually mean for us?"

We stare at him.

"I mean, as a people. How will that change our perception of our lives?"

"In terms of the general population they won't care either way. It's not a concept they can cope with." I say.

"Maybe not. I mean, we've done all the science stuff. Doing. I just... how do you cope with that knowledge that you... we are at every point in our lives at the same time, it's just that our poor mammalian brains are simplifying things into a linear viewpoint to help us cope with it."

"Do you think you're going to go mad again you mean?", Emit smiles at him.

"I think he already is," Petter laughs, "Mad as butter, as my mother would say."

"Hah, yeah thanks, been there done that twice as we all know. Never again. Emit though, come on, surely you've thought about more than the scientific implications of this... your experiment?"

Emit gazes to nothing for a few seconds, before pushing his plate towards the middle of the table. He places a meatball at one edge.

"This is you."

"Mackie is a rehydrated meatball! That's his brain on all that medication!" We laugh.

"If time is linear, you are moving clockwise around the outside of the plate, seeing time progressing forwards in your direction of travel. The outcome of events is unknown until the event happens."

This is school-grade level stuff, but Emit has them glued, waiting for some profound pay-off. I decide to finish my meal before I regress to a childlike state.

"But if time isn't linear, then we are everywhere on the outside of the plate at the same time." He places more meatballs. "This means that theoretically it should be possible for all meatball Mackies to perceive the states of all the others at the same time."

"Which is the point of this... your experiment. Except we're using laser energy sources instead of meatballs and a singularity warping spacetime instead of a plate."

"Exactly. But change human perceptions? Why not? Every scientific discovery allows us to look at our universe differently. Why should it not be possible for everyone to perceive time differently also? Just imagine, the course of human history will never be the same again, as there would *be* no history!"

Petter looks at the plate thoughtfully. "We see time progressing forwards. It may or may not be non-linear, but couldn't it also be possible to perceive time in reverse? Meatball walking backwards?"

"Whoa", Mackie puts his hands up. "That would be a screwed-up life. Worse than mine!"

"How so?" Emit leans forwards intently.

"Living life backwards in linear time, you'd always be seeing the effects of events you had no awareness of your input into. You would be scrutinising every element of your conscious moment to try to make sense of what you've already done... were about to do. You'd just want to end it! At least I would."

My scraping chair interrupts them as I get up. "Well, before our 'enlightenment', we've still to crunch numbers and get to 100% power output."

"Ah Cheryl, such spite in your voice. But when the enlightenment comes, when all calculations are meaningless and your destiny is laid out before you, what then for you?"

"Same as you Emit, I'll be out of a job."

***

The chamber reverberates fiercely. My muscles shiver inside my skin and my vision shifts. A glow I hadn't even noticed fades from the room as the screens confirm matter input has ceased.

"Tango-Foxtrot Two to Omega Control. 96% power cycle complete."

Console readings appear. Branch one-hundred and eighteen. "That was 92.11% correlation with just your default coordinates. And the correlation increase is no longer linear with power input as you predicted Emit. We could even start seeing potential interference patterns from other time states before we reach full power."

"We'll be mush before we get any higher. These distortions worse than you predicted." Petter shakes his head. "We are still 'safe distance' yes?"

"The sphere has been designed to contain well over the required gravitational distortion. You know that as well as I, now stop being so theatrical."

He huffs angrily at my comment.

Emit, calm as ever, strokes his keypad. "Yes, we're fine. We'll get the correlation. Two more runs and we're there."

***

Petter grabs a chair next to me and Emit over break-
fast.

"Next cycle soon Cheryl! Excited yes?"

"I'm looking forward to the results to see if they
match Emit's predictions..."

"Ah come on girl, some enthusiasm! We could be
about to stare God in the face."

I shake my head strongly. "Don't even bring that
into the conversation Petter. It won't end well. Trust
me."

"Hah. I know you don't believe. But the nature of
the universe is everything. Just as He is. Who knows, if
they are one and the same, then it'll be an interesting
experiment yes? Love to see your write-up of that
one!"

"Petter, if God does pop out of my sphere to say
'Hi', I won't be on his contact list. You know that I
can't reconcile the thought that everything is preor-
dained."

"So that's why you don't like Emit's talk. If time is
non-linear you won't be queuing up for enlightenment
eh?"

Emit smiles to himself. I watch Petter shovel his meal down. I've lost my appetite.

"You know what my mother always said..." Here we go, another famous anecdote. "We're all playthings Petter, pulled by invisible strings, we just can't see it."

Something clicks into place in my brain, and I suddenly feel oddly overwhelmed. I get up quickly to try and shake the sensation. "Cycle in eight guys. Got to prepare."

***

"Tango-Foxtrot Two to Omega Control. You have 98% power. Starting cycle in T-minus fifty seconds."

Mackie scans the beam trajectories and temperatures. Petter carefully watches half a dozen EM shield screens as matter is poured into the sphere. I keep my eye on the structural sensors, waiting for the zero. I glance over at Emit. He's silent as always, but not looking at his screens any more. Instead he's staring at the sphere.

"Magnetic shield holding. Matter inputs full injection. Cycle starting."

The chamber starts to resonate as we hit zero. I'm at branch sixty-one.

Almost immediately I see a full correlation. Impossible! Not with this power input. But there they are, interference patterns from our future selves. The room is glowing again. Something isn't right. I move my hand to touch the screen and it moves jerkily, like waves of water are pushing it back. This isn't gravitational distortion, no alarms are going off. That could only mean some unforeseen factor affecting my perception. How could we have missed this? How do we operate the experiment if this effect continues? We must abort. Path five from branch sixty-one. I go to start shut-down procedure and look around for Emit to confirm. He is standing right in front of the observation window arms stretched out wide, fingers splayed as if feeling the wind blowing over him. He calmly turns around and looks at me, smiling like a child.

"You my girl, what's your name?"

"Cheryl. But..."

"Well this is where it all begins Cheryl. I have planned this moment for so long, yet I have everything to learn about how I got here."

The distortions are hitting me like a physical force now. My vision skews and pops. "Emit, we must abort..."

"Your future is good, you will see everything. And me? My mind will no longer be trapped, freefalling backwards to my birth."

No! What's he done? I can't control my muscles any more, I can barely see. I feel like I'm floating out of my chair as my body pulses with the universe, then everything goes black.

***

"Awake child, awake. My life is just beginning and you will never see yours in the same way again. Open your eyes and awake."

I open my eyes and see all the colours of Jupiter flowing through time.

ABOUT THE AUTHOR

Hello there,

Thanks for buying and reading my short stories. I would love to hear your thoughts on them, so please feel free to contact me using the information overleaf. Also, I would be very grateful if you could leave a review wherever you purchased this collection from, as it helps immensely.

If you liked these stories, then you may also like my full-length novels POWERLESS and the sequel KILLING GODS. They are dark superhero thrillers set in an alternate version of Britain. They are available digitally everywhere, and as paperbacks on Amazon via Createspace. I am currently writing the third book in the series, with a fourth planned.

Thanks again for reading,
Tony.

My blog

www.hungryblackbird.com

Facebook

www.facebook.com/TonyCooperAuthor

Twitter

@_tonycooper

Email

tonycooperauthor@gmail.com

Amazon

amazon.com/author/tonycooper

Smashwords

www.smashwords.com/profile/view/TonyCooper

Goodreads

www.goodreads.com/user/show/7234993

OTHER TITLES

When the best friend of a retired superhero is killed by another power, Martin must drag himself out of his self-imposed isolation to find out who is responsible. In doing so he finds himself digging up a past he would rather forget, risking exposing the secret of why the team split up and destroying all their lives in the process.

When the baby son of a physically mutated eighties villain goes missing from protective care, he goes on a rampage to try and find him.

In his way stand a Child Protection Officer following her heart above her duty, a violent anti-hero group desperate for media attention, a seemingly benevolent hero-worshipping cult and Martin and Hayley struggling to work out who they can trust.

Printed in Great Britain
by Amazon